NO PLACE TO HIDE

HARPER ASHLEY
WREN HAWTHORNE

Cover Design by Harper Ashley

Formatting & Interior Design by Harper Ashley / The Havoc Archives

Editing by The Havoc Archives

Sensitivity Reading by The Havoc Archives

Blurb by The Havoc Archives

First Edition 2023

Dedication

For all you dirty little sluts out there who like your book boyfriends a little unhinged... ready to have some fun?

-Harper

You liked being called a dirty little slut, huh?

-Wren

Content Warning

This book is intended for those over the age of 18. This book contains graphic scenes and explicit sexual content. The actions depicted in this book may be dangerous and are strictly a work of fiction. *Reader discretion is advised.*

Trigger Warnings

anal, barebacking, blood play, bondage, claustrophobia, clowns, consensual non-consent, confinement play, degradation, edging, fear play, gagging, humiliation, impact play, knife play, mask kink, masochism, mention of the death of a loved one, mention of murder, oral sex, pet names, praise, primal play, public play, rough sex, sadism, sexually explicit scenes, snowballing, spanking, spitting, tribbing, voyeurism, vulgar language

Contents

PRECAUCION

playlist
MIND GAMES - SICKICK
YOU PUT A SPELL ON ME - AUSTIN GIORGIO
SUCH A WHORE - JVLA
CIRCUS PSYCHO - DIGGY GRAVES
DARKSIDE - NEONI
CHILLS (DARK VERSION) - MICKEY VALEN, JOEY MYRON
DESIRE (SLOWED) - PCX THOUSAND
DO IT FOR ME - ROSENFELD
HOTEL - MONTELL FISH
TEAR YOU APART - SHE WANTS REVENGE

Chapter One

Jackson

The unrelenting sun beats down on me as I pull another metal beam from the back of a rusted tractor trailer, sweat dripping down the back of my neck. It's hot for October. Too fucking hot.

I can't stand the South.

In a few short hours these beams will stand over thirty feet tall, the massive red and white canvas of the big top tent cascading around them like a cloak of mystery for all to see.

Becoming a carny wasn't exactly a lifetime ambition of mine, but criminal records make your options dwindle to nothing.

"Hey, pretty boy, you got them beams out yet?"

I also can't stand the local nobodies we hire on for the two weeks we stay in each town. He looks like he's less than a half hour away from sneaking into a port-a-potty for his next fix. He's not the first to call me pretty boy, though it typically only takes one time for them to never want to make that mistake again.

Even under all the sweat and dirt I still attract people like a magnet. It's always the ones who want nothing to do with other people, isn't it?

I bear down on my teeth, gritting them tightly together so I don't say something that ends with me back in Sylvester's office getting my ass chewed. I have a tendency to write checks with my mouth that my fists have to cash later.

The last of the beams clang loudly against the others when I drop it, the sound of metal hitting metal the only response he gets.

"Careful, Mac. That one's testy," Hank calls over his shoulder with a chuckle.

Hank is probably the only person in this place I can stand, and even that's debatable sometimes. He's twice my age and always drunk, but decidedly less stupid than the rest of these fuckers.

I shoot a warning glance over at Mac, and unsurprisingly, he backs down. A bead of sweat collects over my lip and I wipe it away with the back of my arm.

My eyes train onto the shitty trailer I call home, the cold shower inside calling my name louder and louder with each passing second I stay in this heat.

"You draw a straw yet?" Hank asks when he comes to my side, his voice sounding more throaty than normal, probably due to the endless cigarettes he smokes.

I shake my head.

The people here always rush to draw straws as soon as we land in a new place. I could care less what job I get stuck with.

I've done it all by now, and they all suck.

"What did you get?" I ask.

He pulls a soft pack of cigarettes from his back pocket and sticks one in between his teeth. "Fucking kiddie coaster."

I take it back. All the jobs do suck, but the ones where you get trapped around screaming children are the worst.

"At least I can chat up the hot moms while their snot goblins ride. You may wanna go draw, kid. Livestock is still up for grabs and we both know how much you love shovelin' shit."

No one else really likes that one, but I don't mind it. It's quiet and I don't have to deal with the public.

I shrug. "Maybe I'll volunteer."

"And miss out on all these sweet Southern belles the glorious South has to offer? Fuck off. Go get your straw."

Hank knows good and damn well I don't occupy my time with the miserable women who throw themselves at the few of us worth looking at for a night of meaningless fun.

I'm not fucking interested.

“Only a few are still up for grabs,” Sylvester says after taking a long drag off the cheap cigar wrapped in his fat fingers. “Gino put his up for trades if you’re interested. He got concessions again.”

I reach into the brown paper bag and pull my straw.

It’s not really a straw.

It’s a small torn piece of notebook paper covered in the boss’s chicken-scratch handwriting.

“Keepin’ it or taking the trade?”

I stuff the small scrap of paper into my pocket and turn, giving Sylvester my back. “Nah. Keepin’ it.”

It’s my favorite. I know I said they all suck, but this one just happens to suck the least.

Our only dark attraction, Shifty’s Fun House. Perfect for Halloween.

A dilapidated haunted house on wheels with a massive clown head for the entrance. When you step into his open mouth you’re met with complete darkness, creepy circus music, and the stench of poorly maintained upholstery.

There’s jump scares by shitty animatronics and enough strobe lights to make anyone feel like they’re seconds away from seizing.

It’s not grade A horror by any means, but in the dark anything can be terrifying.

It even has one of those trippy spinning tunnels that mimic the same sensation as taking too much LSD.

When you near the end of the fun house you meet our very own Shifty the Clown, clad in torn ruffles and splattered with fake blood.

He pops out of the pitch-black darkness when you round the final corner, robotic eyes glowing red with murderous rage.

The screams make for an entertaining evening.

I stalk toward my trailer without speaking to anyone, including Hank as he calls out for me to join their poker game under the tent.

All I can think about is that cold shower and my head hitting the pillow.

Gates open at noon tomorrow, and the first day is always a packed house.

Chapter Two

Blair

"This place smells like clogged arteries and sweat."

I roll my eyes and keep walking down the breezeway, passing the various stands and food trucks offering everything from funnel cake to Italian ice.

"I want one of those lemonades," I say, gesturing toward a small yellow cart.

"There's no telling what they put in that shit. Drink at your own risk. I'll stick to bottled water. If you're going to drag me around this cesspool, I at least want to survive it. You seriously couldn't think of a better way to spend Halloween?"

"Mallory, I love you, but Jesus are you wound up tighter than Mrs. Sharpton's girdle. What? Would you rather be trick-or-treating with your little sister and her friends?"

My best friend lets out a dramatic groan. "Are the guys here already?"

I shrug. "No clue. Travis said they were coming tonight. You know how they are, though."

A lanky man with a faded butterfly tattoo on his neck is positioned behind the counter of the lemonade cart.

"What size?" he asks, looking me up and down.

"You can't be serious," Mallory whispers under her breath, and I drive my elbow into her side.

"Small, please."

The man reaches for a small plastic cup and positions it under the nozzle.

"That'll be five bucks."

I reach inside my bag and pull out my small change purse. "You sure you don't want one?" I ask her, and she narrows her eyes.

I turn my attention back to the man and hand him the bill in exchange for the cup.

"Wanna ride the Ferris wheel? Or maybe the thing that spins over there?"

Mallory scoffs. "If you think I am getting on any of these death traps you've got another thing coming. I didn't survive finals week just to end it all at some dirty carnival. I will be keeping my feet planted firmly on the ground instead of being tossed around like veggies in a food processor."

Our experience couldn't be more different.

Growing up I never got to come to places like this. Traveling carnivals weren't exactly a place frequented by people like my parents. They were more likely to be found at galas supporting some obscure charity or country club.

This place is sensory overload and I'm enjoying every single second of it.

The rides are luminous against the dark sky, flashing lights and colors dancing above our heads. A claw shaped ride hurtles through the air, the legs of those brave enough to get on dangling wildly as they get slung back and forth.

"There's a mirror maze over there," I say, pointing toward the back of the carnival where a row of indoor attractions sit.

"That seems safe enough," Mallory responds, not a trace of amusement lacing her words.

"Look who it is," a familiar voice coos in my ear as an arm slides over my shoulder.

Travis.

He's wearing too much cologne—the expensive one his mom got him last Christmas.

"Here I am," I mutter under my breath, but he doesn't seem to notice. He's too busy marking his territory, making sure that everyone around me knows that even though we broke up last month, he still views me as his.

I've yet to go on even one ride because Mallory flat out refuses, and now my ex will make sure that I don't leave his sight for the rest of the night.

So much for enjoying my evening at the carnival.

"Blair, can we talk?" he asks, arm tightening around me.

I shrug out from underneath him and shake my head. "Not here, Travis."

I'm not sure why I bother. He's never been great at listening to anything that comes out of my mouth.

"Baby, don't make me beg in front of our friends. I just wanna talk."

Deciding that indulging him is better than causing a scene, I relent.

I allow him to lead me toward a secluded area but try not to stare too long at the giant clown face to our left.

The words Shifty's Fun House are blinking above the monstrosity, though I'm not convinced there is anything *fun* inside.

"How long are you going to make me play along with this whole 'taking a break' bullshit?"

I don't know how many other ways we can have this exact same conversation.

"We aren't taking a break, Travis. We've broken up. There is no uncertainty hanging above it."

He lets out a groan and places each of his hands on my shoulders, his voice getting louder.

"Look, I've tried to be as understanding as possible. I get that you needed space or whatever, but this shit is getting old. It's been you and me since high school."

That's the problem.

"I don't want to do this now. I came here to have fun, not fight with you. Can we please just—"

His grip on my shoulders tightens and I wince.

"Hey!" a deep voice calls out, and both our heads snap to locate where it came from.

It's the employee taking tickets at the entrance of the fun house. He's seated in a metal folding chair, his black boots propped up on the railing.

"You got a problem, buddy?" Travis calls back to him, and I think I can tell before he can that this guy isn't someone he wants to mess with.

"No problem, buddy." Something wicked drips from his words as he repeats the sentiment back to Travis. "Looks like she has a problem with you grabbing her, though."

I wish I could melt into the ground beneath me. This is mortifying.

"Just stop. Walk away," I plead, trying to tap into whatever recesses of reason are still firing in my ex's primate brain.

"Walk away? That guy just—" he starts, but instead of finishing his sentence, he just throws his hands up and storms off.

I can't make out whatever he's mumbling under his breath as he leaves me standing there, but I don't really care.

I turn back to the man, intent on thanking him for the intervention.

I don't get the chance, though.

The chair is now empty, his Styrofoam cup still placed on the ground beside it.

My brain is screaming at me to go back to Mallory and the others, but my feet are already walking toward the fun house. I'm not sure if I've shut off my own reasoning and am operating on autopilot, but the curiosity about the mysterious man wins out.

He didn't look like any of the other carnival workers I'd seen so far.

He was young, maybe a few years older than me.

His dark hair hung in his eyes, and it wasn't hard to tell that he was a tall guy. His limbs were long but not scrawny, like he'd be able to pick up just about anything without much of a struggle at all.

There aren't many places he could have gone. I would have seen if he'd walked back toward the commotion of the carnival. That left either inside the fun house or behind it.

My money was on the latter, or at least, that's where I hoped he'd gone.

I wasn't exactly jumping at the idea of walking inside the creepy clown mouth.

Chapter Three

Jackson

Behind the fun house is dark and quiet, and I need to take a minute to calm the fuck down before I get myself fired.

The last thing I need is to beat some frat boys ass on the job.

I shouldn't have said anything, but it was obvious the girl was uncomfortable. I'm not entirely sure why I gave a fuck, but by the time I'd had enough time to process what I was seeing I'd already opened my mouth.

"Hey," a small voice fills the dead space around me.

I turn and furrow my brow. "Employees only back here."

She takes a step back, uncertainty painted on her face. "Sorry, I just wanted to thank you."

"Not necessary."

I turn to walk away, already dreading the ass chewing I'll get from Sylvester if he realizes I've left the attraction entrance unguarded.

"It is necessary. You didn't have to speak up."

I exhale and keep walking. "Well, you thanked me. Have a nice night."

"Wait up!" she calls after me, picking up her pace to match mine.

"Look, I don't make it a habit to involve myself in lover's quarrels. I also don't make it a habit to babysit damsels in distress—"

The light from the entrance to Shifty's falls across her face and my words catch in my throat before I can finish whatever asshole sentence that was about to come out of my mouth.

Shit. She's gorgeous.

Her golden hair is gathered in a high ponytail, with a few strands framing her heart-shaped face. Light green eyes that remind me of a meadow of tall grass, and perfectly pink lips.

"Damsel in distress? Seriously?" She plops a hand on her hip and looks at me incredulously. "That makes you... what? My knight in shining armor?"

I shake my head. "No knight here. Just a guy who needs to get back to work."

She surveys the empty railing, noting the lack of patrons.

"Right..." Her tongue clicks against the roof of her mouth. "Because you're *so* busy."

I take a step toward her, expecting her to cower back. When she doesn't, I can feel the slightest tinge of a smile trying to pull at my lips.

She looks so small, with me towering over her.

"What's your name?" she asks in her honey-sweet voice.

I narrow my eyes, not sure how opening my mouth ended up with me making small talk with a pageant princess outside the fun house.

"Jackson," I tell her after a few seconds pass.

A radiant smile appears, and I curse myself for all the things I want to do to her.

All the ways I want to take that sweet, innocent little mouth and make it do horribly dirty things.

"I'm Blair, and the guy you saved me from is my ex. Travis. He isn't taking the breakup well."

"Clearly."

I stuff my hands into my pockets and lean against the railing.

She takes a step toward me. "How in the world did you end up working at a place like this? You don't look like—"

"Like a carnie?" I finish, and she takes her bottom lip into her teeth.

"I didn't mean it in a bad way. I just mean you don't exactly look like you fit in... with the others."

She's carefully choosing her words, trying to not offend me or any potential carnie friends I may have.

"The carnival doesn't do background checks, and most places don't hire people with records like mine."

I see the fear flash in her eyes and my cock twitches in my pants.

She looks up at me, doe eyes beaming with conflict. Her curiosity is exploding but her brain is telling her to walk away.

She *should* walk away.

"Blair!" a voice calls out from across the opening in front of the fun house. "What the hell are you doing?"

A woman barrels toward us, jet black hair down to the middle of her back swinging with each step.

"Talking to my new friend," Blair responds coolly. "This is Jackson. Jackson, this is Mallory."

"Travis is pissed, Blair. I swear there is actual smoke coming out of his ears."

The girl at my side tilts her head upwards and sighs.

"B, let's go. My feet hurt, I'm hungry, and I need at least three showers to wash away the stench of fried food and grime from my body." Her friend looks toward me. "No offense."

"None taken." I respond, my eyes still on Blair.

Blair doesn't move, even when her friend begins to tap her foot impatiently.

"I'm not ready to leave, Mal. I haven't ridden a single ride and I've had my eye on one of those foot-long corn dogs for hours."

She may look like a princess, but this one has some fire to her.

I like that.

"You can't be serious. The guys want Shake Shack and I'm not eating any of this shit here. Can we please just go?"

I watch the wheels spinning in Blair's mind.

"Just go with them. My car is in the lot."

Her friend's head is seconds away from spinning on its axis like something from The Exorcist.

"I am not leaving you here, alone, with this weird dude. We have that party tonight, remember? We're supposed to be going as angels! What the hell is going on with you, B?"

"No offense, right?" I ask, one corner of my mouth curled into a smirk. I allow the image of Blair dressed as a sexy angel to fill my mind.

"You know what? No. Full offense meant. Blair, let's go!" When she doesn't move from her position at my side Mallory lets out an exasperated groan. "When he kidnaps you, and you end up on the side of a milk carton, don't fucking call me, B."

With that, she storms off and leaves the two of us standing there.

"Should I be worried about getting kidnapped, Jackson? You mentioned a criminal record."

I laugh. “Not at all, princess.”

I wait a few beats before speaking again.

“Unless you’re into that kind of thing.”

TICKET
8172205
MACO TAG & LABEL
KEEP
THIS
COUPON
8172205

Chapter Four

Blair

My entire body is blaring with alarm bells.

Somehow I feel both completely safe *and* in imminent danger with Jackson.

"It's dark and quiet back here. I could snatch you up and take you. I doubt anyone would hear your screams over the rides."

My mouth drops open, shock over his words written all over my face.

"That was a joke."

I nod, but don't close my mouth.

"You really should go with your friends, though. Closing is soon and there are shady fucks around here who won't be joking when they scoop you up."

My heart thumps in my ears and my cheeks flame with heat. "You wouldn't let that happen."

Jackson's gaze narrows, his dark eyes giving away nothing as he stares at me.

"You sure do have a lot of faith in strangers, B."

The use of my nickname sends a wave of something I can't put my finger on through my body.

We stand there in silence. Neither one of us seems to know what to say next. I shift my weight from one foot to the other and pull a strand of tickets from my bag.

"How many for the fun house?"

Jackson's eyes dart from mine down to the tickets in my hand.

"Two."

I tear off two tickets and hold them out, trying not to hold my breath as I wait for him to react.

He takes them and walks to the entrance. "Enjoy."

I go through the clown's large mouth and am instantly engulfed in darkness, the sound of circus music and distant laughter filling my ears.

The hall is narrow, and I have to hold my hands out at each side to feel for where to go. A loud bang jolts me as a strong spray of air hits me in the face.

"Come one, come all! Step inside my house of horrors."

The recording of a creepy voice plays over busted speakers, words fizzling in and out as the phrase repeats on a loop.

The ground underneath me creaks and gives with each step.

More laughter plays in the distance, and I see the haze from a black light leading me around a corner. A large spinning tunnel greets me, with neon paint that appears to glow splattered haphazardly around. Rails on each side of the wood planks allow me to keep some semblance of balance as I make my way through the tunnel.

On the other side, I see a large stuffed spider propped up against the ceiling, and when a latch releases—sending it flying in my direction—a squeal escapes my lips.

I round a corner and am greeted by a large open room. It's decorated to look like a clown's dressing room. One wall is nothing but mirrors, but most of them are cracked. Another wall is covered in smears of red paint.

The words "*is this what I look like*" appear to have been painted on with someone's fingers.

IS THIS
WHAT I
LOOK LIKE

An antique vanity sits against the other wall, the mirror of it covered by shreds of newspaper.

Several dingy clown costumes hang from a clothing rod.

I pick up my pace, wanting to find the exit as soon as possible.

More puffs of air shoot at me paired with loud bangs that sound like a baseball bat slamming against a metal wall.

I can faintly see the lights from outside.

When I round the final corner, a massive animatronic clown pops out from the darkness and sends me flying into the opposing wall.

Glowing red eyes stare back at me, and I sidestep the creature, feeling for the exit door.

The warm fall breeze hits my face when I'm finally free.

"Was it worth the two tickets?" Jackson asks when I close the door behind me.

"It's definitely a lot scarier being in there alone," I say, turning to face him.

"If that scared you, princess, this place is not somewhere you want to be when the gates close."

He's right.

I look down at my phone to check the time.

11:25 PM.

"Carnival closes at midnight, right?" I ask.

He nods. "But the rides close in five."

The crowd is thinning, and suddenly the reality of being here alone sinks in.

"Do you think... you could walk me to my car?"

Jackson shakes his head. "I can't leave the fun house yet. People like to sneak in."

Why on Earth would anyone want to sneak into that place?

"You'd be surprised how often we catch people trying to fuck in the tunnel," he adds, as if reading my mind.

I scrunch my face up in disbelief. "Who could possibly have sex in that thing? I felt like I was going to fall over just trying to walk through it!"

His eyes go dark and my stomach does a serious of flips.

Thump. Thump.

My heartbeat is in my ears again.

Thump. Thump.

I'm talking about sex with an incredibly hot carnival worker in front of a haunted fun house.

Thump. Thump.

This is so not me. This is not something Blair Fields does.

"You can fuck anywhere if you want it bad enough," he responds, voice low and husky.

Thump. Thump.

"Y-yes. I guess you can."

Jackson steps toward me. He reaches out and takes a loose strand of my hair, twisting it in his fingers.

I swallow the lump in my throat, unable to speak.

He releases the strand of hair but doesn't step back.

"You should go."

His words taunt something inside me that I didn't even know was there. It's something that makes me want to behave in ways I never would have considered before this very moment.

"What if I don't want to?" I ask quietly, scared to break his gaze. Scared that if I do, whatever spell that's currently taking over me will break and I will realize how insane this all is.

Jackson clenches his jaw, considering my question. "I'm not like your frat boy, princess. I wasn't joking about my record. I work in a fucking traveling carnival and live in a shitbox trailer with no hot water." He places his hand under my chin and tilts my face upwards so I'm staring right into his almost obsidian eyes. "Whatever little defiant fantasy you think you're trying to live out by slumming it with me isn't going to end well for you."

Everything he's saying is true.

I know it is.

When someone tells you exactly who and what they are, you should believe them.

But I don't care.

Every fiber of my being is buzzing with need and all I want is for him to keep touching me, to feel his calloused hands against my soft skin.

"Now run along, B."

Chapter Five

Jackson

Something flickers in her eyes when I tell her to go.

All I know is that every second she stands here and doesn't walk away my resolve grows weaker.

"I never act reckless," she finally says. "I was perfect in high school, and now I'm perfect in college. I was captain of the cheer team and dated the quarterback. I've never been with anyone but Travis, and whenever I went to sleep every night all I could think about was how perfectly boring my life was. Always doing the same things with the same people. Eating the same foods, listening to the same songs."

She reaches up and pulls the tie out of her hair and shakes it out, honey colored locks cascading around her shoulders. "I broke up with him because I felt like I was going insane. Perfect Blair in her perfect little box with her perfect little life. Maybe I don't want that. Maybe I want to know what it feels like to do something *bad*."

Uh... huh.

Lights begin to shut off in the area around us, and the sound of the whirring rides die down.

I know I shouldn't do this. Trust me, I do. But the demented bastard I call my cock is screaming for me to take little miss perfect and give her exactly what she's asking for.

So I *have* to do it. Them's the rules.

This should be fun.

"Get inside," I demand.

"What?" she squeaks out, eyes wide and full of shock.

"Go inside and don't come out until I tell you to. Understand?"

She nods, hesitating before taking a step backwards.

"Jackson—"

I hold up a finger. “Blair, I told you to go home. I told you this isn’t where you belong. This is your final warning. You either walk to the gate and leave, or you go inside and wait for me to come back.”

She chews on the inside of her cheek, and I can tell she’s at war with herself over what to do.

“If you *are* still here when I come back, I promise I’ll give you what you want. You wanna stop having to be you for the night? I’ll show you what it's like to be someone else.”

Sylvester has a line of attraction workers in front of him, all waiting to hand over the tickets collected for the night. I don’t know why the hell he wants the damn things, but he says he likes to keep a tally of what’s performing well.

He’s preoccupied, so he won’t notice when I slip away before count out.

Hank slaps a hand on my shoulder. “Crowd wasn’t as big as I expected for an opening night.”

“Yeah,” I mutter, thinking about whether or not I’m going to find Blair where I left her.

“You coming down to play tonight? We’re meeting at my place. I’m going double or nothing. Gotta make up for my shit hands last night.”

“You know the answer to that, Hank. Jackson thinks he’s too good to hang with us,” Tiny calls out over his shoulder.

I’m not sure who decided that behemoth of a man should be called Tiny, but somehow it stuck.

“I’d rather sleep than spend my off-time shooting the shit with you drunks,” I respond flatly. “You all fucking suck at poker anyways.”

I toss my pouch of tickets to Hank and turn on my heel. The keys to Shifty’s are supposed to be in there too, but those are nestled in my pocket.

"I taught your ungrateful ass how to play," Hank yells after me, but I can hear the smile on his face.

"Yeah, and then the student became the master."

My feet thud against the ground as I make the long walk from the big top tent back to Shifty's.

She won't be there.

I picture her standing there when reality came crashing in and she came to her senses. Girls like that don't want to mess around with guys like me. As soon as I left she probably realized how ridiculous all of this is and bolted.

She's probably in her car driving back to her perfect life, and she'll never give the guy from the carnival a second thought ever again.

A part of me considers going straight to the trailer.

Families gather around the rows of rigged carnival games, wasting their time and money on shitty stuffed animals and inflatable aliens.

I should just go home, take a shower, and go to bed.

Forget about her.

When the fun house comes into view my heart rate picks up and my blood feels like fire in my veins. I'm gonna be pissed if I walked all the way over here just to find out she left.

I walk up the two steps that lead to the entrance and grab onto the top of Shifty's mouth, stretching my arms overhead and bracing my weight against it.

I stop to listen for any movement.

Silence.

I let out a deep breath and push off the entrance.

When I turn, a small hand reaches out and wraps around my wrist.

She emerges from the shadows, face still marred with uncertainty. That uncertainty isn't alone, though. There's also a glint of excitement in her eyes.

I twist my wrist around so that it's my hand capturing hers, and I push her back into the darkness. I use my other hand to grasp her free wrist, and pin them both to the wall above her head.

"You sure?" I breathe out, my voice low against her throat.

She nods, and the fires of desire are a molten pit swirling to life inside me.

"You have to tell me to stop if it's too much," I rasp.

She nods again, a whimper escaping her lips as her anticipation builds. I move both of her wrists to one of my hands, keeping her pinned to the wall. My free hand cups her jaw, my thumb pushing its way into her mouth. She opens wide for me, allowing me to press it as far back as I can without gagging her.

I want to take this slow.

Her lips wrap around the base of my finger and suck as I pull it back out.

No, I don't.

"*Fuck.*"

My fingers lightly trace down her skin and she arches underneath my touch. When I reach the button securing her shorts I pull it free with ease. The zipper slides down, and once I have enough room I slip my hand in, cupping her warmth with my palm.

She's already soaking wet.

"Is it really that easy to turn you on, princess? I shouldn't be surprised. Does Travis even know what to do with his dick? Has he ever fucked you the way you deserve to be fucked?"

Blair lets out a delicious whimper and my cock twinges in response.

"That's right," I grit through closed teeth into her ear as I sink two fingers deep into her wetness.

I release her wrists and tangle my fingers in her hair, fisting the locks and tilting her head to the side. My mouth descends on hers, capturing her moans as my other hand continues to thrust in and out of her pussy.

There was nothing gentle or sweet about what I was doing.

"For tonight," I breathe out as I pull away from her mouth, "This is mine."

I pull my fingers out and plunge them back in.

"All I can give you is one night, but we can make it one that you will never forget."

She jolts underneath me, nodding in agreement.

"Say it, princess. Tell me it's all mine."

Blair bucks her hips. “Y-yours. It’s yours.”

Chapter Six

Blair

Jackson pulls his fingers out of me and releases my hair from his grasp. His large palm wraps around my throat and a mixture of fear and excitement pulses through me. A guttural sound escapes my lips as he applies just enough pressure to intensify the buzzing need building within me.

"When you're alone," he begins, his free hand cupping my cheek gently. It's a sharp contrast to the rough grip he has on my throat. "Do you touch yourself?"

My cheeks flame.

I nod, unable to speak.

"Show me." I hesitate, and his grip tightens. A warning to obey. "Show me how you touch yourself when no one else is watching."

I've never been so terrified, but nothing has ever come close to turning me on as much as this gorgeous man and his demands.

I want to please him.

I bring my hand down slowly, keeping my gaze locked onto him. My fingers find my swollen clit and begin to rub it in tiny circles. It doesn't take long for my body to respond. It's like thousands of electric dominoes being lined up and if I keep going, they will all fall.

I can't focus on anything else but his eyes and the way he's watching me, drinking in my euphoric state. I insert a finger, then another. My breath quickens and my eyes begin to flutter as the orgasm builds.

I take my bottom lip between my teeth, my feet nearing the edge of an invisible cliff.

"I-I'm close," I whimper between choppy breaths.

Jackson strokes my cheek, his grasp on my throat still holding strong. He doesn't utter a single word, only watches me with an intensity unlike anything I've ever experienced.

My toes hang over the ledge, and when my fingers return to my swollen bud I finally leap. I fall face first into a pile of tingling ecstasy.

He releases me as my body shudders against him.

"Good, princess. You look so pretty when you come."

My spent body goes limp, one of Jackson's arms wrapping around the small of my back to keep me on my feet.

I should be embarrassed.

I should feel ashamed for what I've just done in front of a man who is basically a stranger.

But I don't.

It feels like I'm riding a high that I don't ever want to come back down from.

"I wanted your first orgasm to be your own." His voice sounds muffled, my ears still ringing from the release. "The rest will be on my terms."

The calluses on his hands feel strange against the softness of my own.

He leads me further into the darkness of the fun house, my heart pounding against my chest with each step.

"So when you say the rest will be on your terms," I finally ask, my voice soft. "What did you mean?"

With the power cut to the place I can't see him in front of me, only feel his hand in mine. He releases it, and I am completely engulfed by the darkness.

With my sight taken from me even the slightest noise is amplified. Each time his boots hit the floor beneath us I shudder.

"Jackson?" I whisper, somehow the absence of light making my own voice seem too loud.

"Let's play a game," he finally says, and I turn.

I am completely disoriented, my senses working overtime to compensate for the sudden loss of vision.

I try to keep my voice steady, but my response is more of a stammer.

"W-what kind of game?"

I have no clue what I have gotten myself into, but it seems far too late to turn back now.

The hair is brushed from my shoulders and I tense, the anticipation from not knowing what will happen next building like a volcano ready to erupt at any moment.

"As a kid, my favorite game was hide and seek." Jackson sounds like he's in front of me now. I reach my hands out but there's nothing there. "I always got a thrill out of hunting. Tracking people down in the dark while they hoped I wouldn't find them."

It sounds like he's all around me. His voice is low and heady. I can almost feel the hunger dripping from his words, something dark and depraved lacing them.

My heart pulsates with fear.

"You want to play hide and seek?" I ask, my voice shaky and unsure.

Jackson didn't strike me as a schoolyard game kind of guy, but something deep in my gut tells me this isn't any ordinary game.

No, this will be something completely different.

The floor creaks and my attention shoots to the direction it came from.

"No, actually, I think *you* want to play hide and seek." I can tell he's moving closer. "There are only three rules. The first is, don't leave the carnival."

I should call this off. Leave this place and never turn back.

"Don't get caught. Not by me, or anyone else."

This is wrong. Twisted.

"If you get caught," he pauses, lingering on the silence. "You get punished."

The world spins around me, like I've stepped onto one of those metal death traps outside. It spins and spins and the silence is deafening. All I can hear is my heart pulsating with fear at the thought of this man chasing me.

"*Punished?*" I squeak, unable to form a coherent sentence.

Jackson's arms envelop me, so tight around my waist it's hard to breathe. He feels so hard behind me, like a wall of solid steel.

His skin is hot, fire against my cool terror.

"I'll give you a head start," he growls into my ear. "Three minutes, Blair."

I've had nightmares that started out like this. A monster has me in their clutches and I break free, running for my life, pleading with the gods to save me.

This isn't a nightmare though, and this monster is very much real.

There is no waking up from this.

The scariest part is that I'm not sure I would want to wake up.

Fear. Intrigue. Need.

My hunter releases me, shoving me away from his reach.

"Time starts now, princess."

My feet are cemented to the floor, my mind and body still at war over whether or not to do this.

"Jackson—" I start, but his voice grows louder in the darkness and my entire being tenses.

"Run," he growls, sounding more like a feral animal than a man.

The ground shakes under my pounding steps.

I slam into a wall, not knowing where the hell the exit is.

Don't look back.

I feel my way down the fabric covered sides, not caring when something sharp bites at the flesh on my hands.

Light outlines my salvation when I finally reach the door that leads back outside.

Don't stop.

I take the steps that lead down from the fun house two at a time, and when my shoes hit the grass, I do exactly as I was told.

I fucking run.

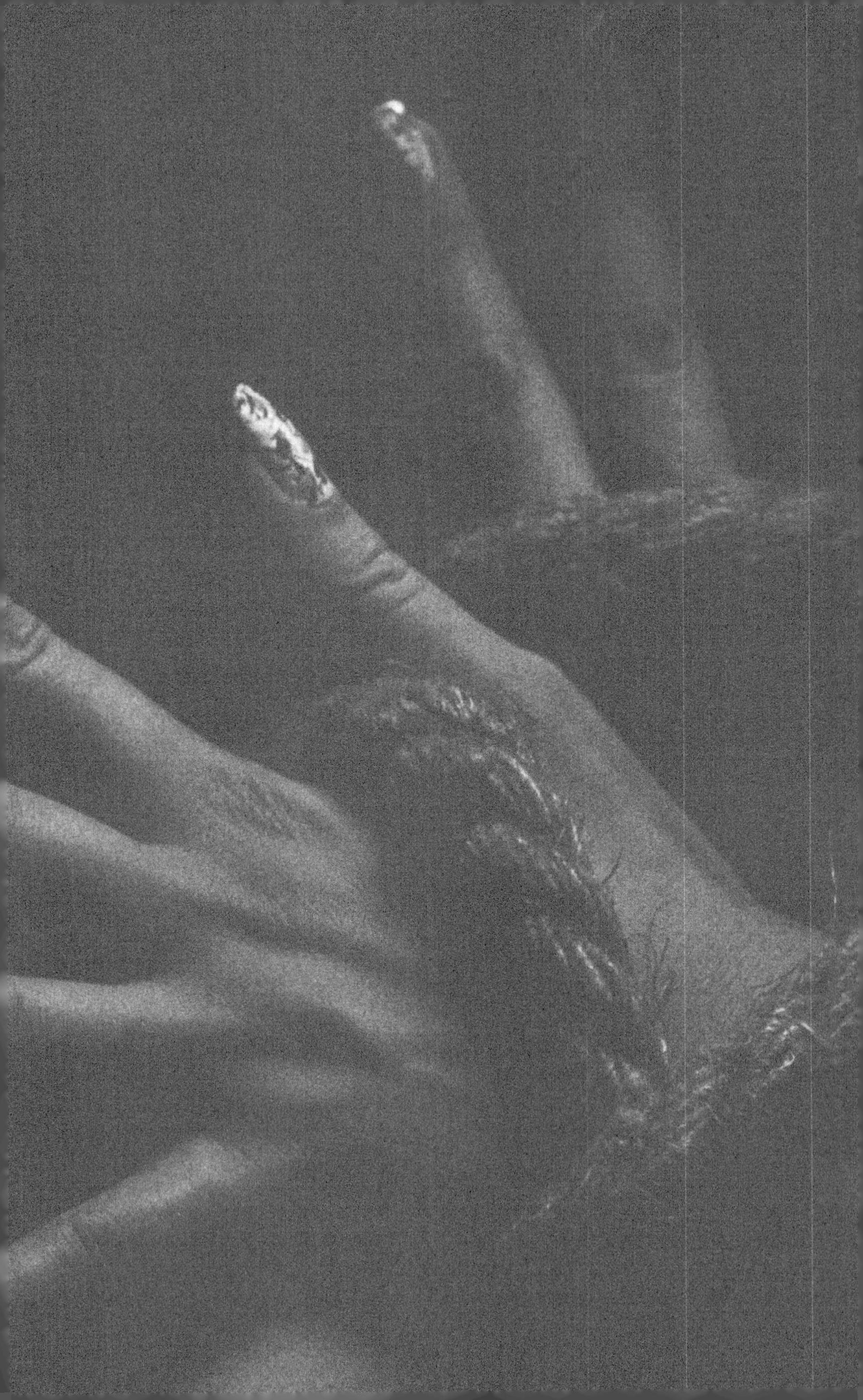

Chapter Seven

Jackson

I probably should've asked what her limits were. It didn't occur to me that she might be new to this. But with the way her hair felt wrapped around my fist, and the sound of her breath coming out in short gasps, the only thing on my mind was the game.

I can hear her footsteps getting further away.

There's only so many places for her to run.

She doesn't know the carnival like I do.

It won't take long for me to find her, if I can't catch up first.

Thirteen...

Fourteen...

I clench and unclench my fists, itching to run my hands over her soft skin.

Fifteen...

Sixteen...

My fingers around her throat while my other hand is between her thighs.

Seventeen...

Her screaming my name.

Eighteen...

Fuck it. That should be enough time.

Rule #4: Don't trust a word that comes out of my mouth.

Alright, princess. Let's play.

I exit the fun house, my eyes scanning every inch of my surroundings. She couldn't have gotten far.

The stench of the carnival wafts toward me, a mixture of sweat and funnel cake. My eyes catch on a glimpse of sun-kissed hair right before it turns a corner.

Got her.

I make my way down the stairs, navigating between all the people milling around. There's kids yelling for popcorn and cotton candy, couples making sure everyone looks at their blatant displays of affection, teenagers looking to prank others. I tune all of it out, solely focused on hunting Blair.

They'll all be gone soon enough, and I'll have my playground all to myself.

I shoulder my way past the food stalls, coming to a stop at the corner I saw her last. The closest place to hide around here is the stable. I slowly make my way over, trying to give it enough time to where she thinks she might have a chance. There's a petting zoo here, with baby animals for the kids to *ooh* and *aah* over. I pick out a kid wearing a baseball cap from the small crowd.

"Hey, kid. You see a woman run through here? Freckles, long hair, pretty?"

"How tall is she?"

What kind of question is that?

"Uh..." I raise my hand right below my chest. "About here?"

The kid shakes his head. I think I may have gotten it wrong, until I hear a small giggle. I whip my head around to see a little girl standing behind me.

"You see her?" I ask.

She giggles again, and I see a few bills crumpled in her fist.

That's how we're playing? Dirty cheater.

"How much did she give you?"

"Five bucks," she answers, holding out her hand to show me.

"I'll double it." She points to the far corner of the stable, where a large pile of hay sits. I reach in my pocket, pulling out a ten, and put it in her hand. "Thanks."

I make my way over to the hay pile, ready to get my hands on Blair. I give it a gentle nudge with my foot. A few seconds pass.

"Blair," I warn. "If I have to come in there, you're going to regret it."

I wait, but nothing happens. I shove my hand inside, expecting to grab her wrist, but all I come out with is a fistful of hay. *What the hell?*

I dig around, leveling the hay until there's no way I can deny she's not fucking here. I turn around to see the little girl wiggling her fingers at me before she skips away.

She scammed me.

I want to *kill* that kid.

I'm covered in hay, and pissed off, but impressed. Blair's not making it easy for me. I like that.

I trudge my way out of the huge mess I made, thinking about where the hell she could be. One of the rides? Ferris wheel? Haunted house?

I'm just about to exit the stable when I see it. The ladder leading up to the loft. Why didn't I think of this before giving that little scammer my last ten bucks? Who taught her that? Where the fuck are her parents?

I raise my head, seeing fresh scuff marks on the ladder, like someone was rushing to get up there. A slow smile creeps across my face. I start the climb up the ladder, making sure my foot doesn't hit the spots where the wood creaks. Peeking my head over the floor of the loft, I look around. Everything looks the same, the bags of feed and hay bales still where I left them earlier.

I don't trust it.

I walk up the last few rungs, standing above the crowd surrounding the petting zoo. Good thing the carnival is about to close. I don't know how I feel about fucking above a bunch of kids.

I don't move, just listen. I focus on keeping my breath quiet, cocking my head when I hear a scuffle. It could be a rat looking for food. There's a small *thump* and a louder, "Fuck."

Yeah, it's a rat. A really big one.

I creep toward the bags of feed. She's sitting down, her back to me, rubbing her elbow.

"Hurt yourself?" I ask, her head turning so fast I'm surprised she didn't give herself whiplash. She gasps, attempting to scurry away from me. I grab her ankle before she can, pulling her back toward me. She flips onto her back, kicking her legs out.

"You cheated!" she says as she looks around, trying to find a way to escape. "That couldn't have been three minutes!"

I'm too focused on trying to avoid her kicking my balls to answer. She's flinging her legs everywhere, like a goddamn donkey. Even her fucking shoes fly off. As soon as I catch her left leg, the right one kicks me in the shin. She freezes.

"You're going to regret that," I say, my eyes darkening.

She squeaks, and I drop to my knees. I pin her wrists above her head, my face hovering over hers.

"That wasn't three minutes," she insists, her voice no louder than a whisper.

"Does it matter?" I ask.

"You're not following the rules."

"Rule #4."

"You said there were three rules!"

"Did I?"

I run my nose along the side of her face. Her breath hitches.

"Y-Yes. You did."

"Huh. Well, I guess you shouldn't trust strangers. Haven't you ever heard of stranger danger?"

"If you don't play by the rules, then there's no game."

"Says who? You? You seem to have been misinformed that you're the one in charge here, sweetheart. Did you already forget paying off that little girl? Looks like neither of us care much about cheating to get our way."

I keep her wrists trapped in one hand as I snake the other down her body, stopping right before I reach the hem of her shorts. My mind is muddled with thoughts of all the things I want to do to her. But first, fair's fair.

I yank her shirt up, pulling it over her head and tossing it to the side. Before she can think to escape, I unclasp her bra and toss it over my head before gathering her wrists back in my hand. I hear a faint, "Hey! Who threw that?"

She doesn't seem to notice and squirms, but she's just rubbing against me, which isn't helping her case.

"Stop moving," I say, before lowering my mouth to her nipple and sucking it hard. She lets out a harsh gasp, and I move to the other nipple while unbuttoning her shorts. I yank them off and stop to look down at her body.

She's curvy yet defined, with a perky ass that fits perfectly in my hands and muscular thighs that could crush my skull. I definitely would enjoy it if she tried to. She's wearing black panties that look like they were part of a set, not that I noticed what her bra looked like.

I flick my tongue over her nipple again while I slip my hand between her thighs. She's soaking wet. I rub her over her panties, and her hips buck involuntarily.

"Fuck..." she breathes, watching me. I alternate between each of her breasts, giving them the attention they deserve as I continue stroking her. Her moans get louder as she moves, trying to make her orgasm come faster. Right when she looks like she's about to be pushed over the edge, I stop. Her head snaps up and she's fucking gorgeous with murder in her eyes.

"What the hell?" she asks, panting.

"Aw, did you forget rule #3?"

"Rule number..." she stops. "No, no, no. Not right now. Come on!"

I start stroking her again, slower this time.

"You can't—"

"Blair, shut up or you're going to get us caught."

I cover her mouth with mine, and she opens for me easily. I sweep my tongue past her plush lips. She tastes like a candied apple and all I want to do is sink my teeth into her. Moving my lips down to her jaw, her neck, her collarbone—I rip her underwear off and plunge two fingers inside of her. Her back arches as she moans—loud enough that I think someone might hear—as I press my thumb to her clit. Her mouth is wide open, and I think about shoving something in there to keep her quiet until her legs start shaking. I stop again, pulling my fingers from her and sucking them into my mouth.

"Damn, you taste good." Her glassy eyes are on me, watching as I lick my fingers. She looks spent, and somewhat defeated.

My grip on her wrists tighten and she lets out a breath. "This is cruel."

"You haven't seen cruel yet, princess. This is just the beginning."

She groans, trying to twist her body away from me.

"Maybe you should try begging."

Her eyes widen in shock. "What?"

"Beg."

She opens and closes her mouth, trying to form words.

"Try... please."

"Please."

"No."

She lets out an exasperated whine. She's clearly growing frustrated with her situation. "You just said to say please!"

"I said try. You tried and failed. Try again."

"Please, let me come."

"Better."

"Please... let me come... uh, please?"

"You're fucking awful at this." I move my jean-clad knee between her legs, pressing it against her core, and lift her leg over my hip. "What, the pretty cheerleader never had to beg for anything before?"

She bites her lip, rubbing herself against me. Her eyes start to roll back in her head, and I know the fabric of my jeans is offering her the friction she's been craving. I let her approach the edge one more time before I yank her back, making her cry out in a way that almost makes it sound painful. Releasing her wrists, I stand, offering her a hand to pull her up with me.

"Stand there," I tell her, pointing to the edge of the loft. The carnival is about to close, and the last few people are shuffling out of the barn, looking to go home.

Her eyes widen. "No way."

I grab her jaw, bringing her face close to mine, my fingers digging in hard.

"I said, stand there. Not 'please', not 'if you want to'. Stand. There." I release her, pushing her toward the edge. She turns, shuffling forward. I reach down to grab a coil of rope lying next to a hay bale. We use a pulley system to haul materials up here. It's about to come in real handy.

"More."

She whines a little bit, but her feet move until she's standing where I want her, looking down at the petting zoo. I move behind her, turning her toward me before grabbing her wrists and tying rope around each of them. I tie a knot around the rope I left hanging between her wrists. I tug on it, making sure the knot holds and she can't escape.

"What are you doing?" she asks.

Ignoring her question, I reach above us and pull down the hook hanging there.

I slip the rope hanging between her wrists around the hook, and tug twice to check the hold. I look at Blair, but she's busy looking at her predicament. She's trying to roll her wrists, but the rope is too tight for her to do much of anything. I can see that she's nervous. She's thinking about how dangerous this is. She doesn't know that this is going to be the safest part of the night. I turn her to face the edge again before moving toward the back wall, and using the pulley to lift her arms above her head, then lift her body until her toes are barely brushing against the ground.

I come up behind her, running my hand down her back, then grab her hips and pull her into me. She rubs her ass against me, and I reach around her, hands squeezing her breasts while my lips find her throat. Her head falls back against me, and that's when she really starts begging.

"I want you so bad..." I unbuckle my belt, shove my jeans down, and bend her over as much as she can go. "I need you inside of me right—"

"Shh, princess. Don't worry. I'll give your body exactly what it's asking for."

I fist my cock, slipping it between her legs. I rub the head against her pussy, drenching it in her. Slowly up and down, up and down, until she starts losing her mind. She gyrates and rubs against me as much as possible until her body starts vibrating.

"Jackson—" she gasps.

I shove my cock inside of her before she can finish her sentence, reveling in the sound of her gasp. She's leaning dangerously over the edge, and if I let her go, she's going over. The only thing that would keep her from falling is the rope.

She's so fucking tight as I continue to thrust into her, not taking care to be gentle. She's enjoying every second of this.

"Yes! More!"

Her eyes are closed, which is probably for the best because she seems like the type to lose her shit over something like this. She's on her tiptoes, back arched, hair falling in front of her face. Keeping one hand on her hip, I slip the other between her legs, stroking her clit as I pound into her. Fuck, she feels good. She's crying out, clenching around my cock, and before I know it she's coming.

I let her ride out her release before easing out of her and flipping her around. Her legs immediately wrap around my waist as I enter her, pumping my hips, our skin smacking against each other. I'm allowing her to be as loud as she wants now that we have some privacy here, and the sounds of the carnival outside are too loud for anyone to hear her screaming.

I forgot about the animals, but who are they gonna tell?

My hands are on her hips, bouncing her on my cock. Her tits are moving in time with our fucking, and I lower my head to quickly take one in my mouth.

"Ah—please don't stop—oh, fuck—you feel so good—"

I feel that familiar heat pool low in my stomach, and her cries are driving me insane.

"You're such a little freak, Blair. How does this feel, being my own personal cum slut? Letting me use your body any way I fucking want." I thrust once more, deep, knowing that's all she needs to shatter apart. "Come for me, princess. Show me how good you feel."

She lets out a low whine as she comes, and I've never seen anything more beautiful than how she looks right now. Breaking apart, hair sticking to her body as she sweats, green eyes ablaze. "Breathe through it, princess. You got it. You're so fucking gorgeous right now. Keep coming for me like a good girl."

Her pussy has my cock in a vise grip, and I follow her right over the edge, shooting deep inside of her. She feels like fucking heaven.

As soon as she starts coming back down from her high, I unwrap her legs from around me and start tucking my dick back in my pants. I walk backwards, watching her legs shake as she tries to hold herself up. I reach the pulley and pull hard, hoisting her up even more. She squeaks from the sudden movement, but is too tired to put up much of a fight. Good.

I return to her, my face directly in line with my target. I settle between her legs, resting her thighs on my shoulders. I trail my hands across her hips and over her ass where I squeeze hard.

"I need something from you, Blair." I lay a kiss on the inside of her thigh.

"Hm?" she mumbles. She's only half here, the other half still in her afterglow.

"I need one more," I say right before licking her pussy. She bucks her hips, crying out.

I know she's feeling oversensitive, but I need this like I need to breathe. I devour her, licking and sucking. It's messy, but just what she needs right now. I trail my hand up her jerking body, taking hold of her tit and kneading her nipple between my fingers. My cum starts to seep from her body into my mouth, and mixes with hers as she comes again, her thighs squeezing my head as her body seizes up. I lick all of our cum up as it comes, holding it in my mouth. I pull her body down, reaching for the rope to help. When her face passes mine, I stop, leaning in to kiss her.

"Open," I command, and she does as she's told. I hold her jaw and spit it all into her mouth. "Swallow."

She does, and I finish pulling her down. I remove her hands from the hook, and untie them. She immediately rubs her wrists. The sight of her raw skin makes my cock twitch. She moves to pick up her clothes, but I swipe them before she can.

"I need those."

"No, you don't. Carnival's closed."

"What about the other carnies?"

"Rule #2."

She reaches for her clothes again. "I can't—hey!" I quickly throw them on the other side of the loft, catching her while she stumbles into me. I grab the back of her neck, smashing my lips into hers. She moans into my mouth, pulling me closer. I nip her bottom lip, and let her go.

"One..."

Chapter Eight

Blair

He begins counting and I don't need to be told what that means.

It's time to run.

I scurry over to the clothes strewn about and grab them into my arms, not bothering to waste a second putting them on. There's no time. I'll just have to pray no one is around to see me running naked through the carnival.

My bare feet slam against the wooden planks of the loft floor, and when I reach the ladder I toss the clothes down. There's no way I can climb down this thing holding them.

Please don't let anyone be down there. Please.

I peer down and see the ground is close, so I hop off the rung and land on my ass.

"Shit!" I cry out, instantly regretting the attention I may or may not have drawn to myself.

I scan the stable and crawl toward my clothes, scraping them into my arms and not giving a shit how filthy they now are thanks to the hay-covered floor.

"Tick tock, princess," Jackson calls out from overhead.

I manage to get back on my feet and pure adrenaline takes over, the fear of being seen suddenly overtaken by the fear of being captured by him.

I run toward the large open doors and round the corner, grateful for the lack of people standing around that were there when I found this hiding place.

I can hear laughter off in the distance, and quickly pivot so that my path goes in the opposite direction.

I have no clue where the hell I am or where I'm going, but I have to find somewhere safe enough to cover myself up.

The smells of the carnival food are still strong enough that I can almost taste it.

I zig-zag through the empty carts and toward one of the kiddie rides. It's five massive metal bears with a hole cut out for people to sit inside. There is a silver wheel in the middle to spin the bears as the ride follows a circular track.

I hurl myself into one of them that is facing the empty parking lot, ducking down to try and hide myself from anyone who may walk by.

I pull on my shirt, then my shorts. My bra must still be in the stable wherever Jackson threw it.

I peek out from the side fully expecting to be caught. It didn't take him long to hunt me down last time, and it's no secret I am at a massive disadvantage.

Jackson knows this place like the back of his hand. Knows every nook and every cranny.

The only way I have a shot at beating him is to outsmart him, and that won't be easy.

Think, Blair. Fucking think!

Returning to the fun house would be too obvious, and heading toward the trailers would be too risky. There is no way I could avoid being caught by one of the carnies.

I need to find somewhere unexpected, somewhere he would never think to look for me.

I run over the layout of the carnival in my mind, trying to think of everything I saw from the moment I arrived to the moment I met Jackson.

I leave the safety of the metal bears and slink into the shadows, keeping close to each of the attractions as I map out potential hiding places.

Something cold and wet jars me from my thoughts and I look down.

The remnants of what I can only hope are spilled soda lay in a puddle at my feet.

My fucking shoes! I left my fucking shoes at the stable.

I scan my surroundings and my eyes narrow in on what seems to be my best bet at losing Jackson.

The game has turned me into someone I don't recognize.

I sprint toward the giant metal fixture that sits at the center of the grounds, gaze locked on the frame. That could easily be climbed.

Well, it may have been easier without the whole *wet and bare* feet issue.

When I reach the Ferris wheel I immediately start my ascent.

I get a few rungs off the ground when my foot slips against the cool metal rod, but my grip on the ones above my head save me.

I keep climbing until I am far enough up that I can see most of the attractions below me, even the dimly lit stable off in the distance.

I steady myself against the frame, sliding my feet to the left a few inches at a time.

Don't look down, don't look down.

A loud bang coming from somewhere behind me makes me freeze in place. I can't breathe and I can't think.

You can do this.

I begin sliding my feet across the metal rod again, getting closer and closer to one of the large covered baskets.

It's bright purple and covered in glitter, the moonlight making it glisten as it reflects off the paint.

I reach out, grabbing for the railing. My hand connects, and I wrap my fingers around it. I pull my weight over the rail and collapse into the basket, hip slamming into the hard bottom.

I lay there curled in a ball, terrified that the slightest movement will make the basket begin to sway again.

If he sees it, I'll be caught.

I squeeze my eyes shut and listen for any noise coming from below me, but all I hear is silence.

Terrifying silence.

I have no clue how much time has passed, but the laughter coming from the area where the trailers are parked has subsided. There hasn't been a single noise, other than the sounds of my own breathing.

An hour? Maybe longer?

My leg has fallen asleep, and I know the second I try to stretch it out the painful sensation of pins and needles will follow.

I try to shift my weight slowly enough that I don't rock the basket.

Easier said than done.

I use my arms to push up, and the sound of the metal hinge securing the basket to the beam overhead makes me want to melt right back into the floor.

Shit. Shit. Shit.

I freeze, praying the noise wasn't noticeable from the ground.

The anticipation is enough to send my nerves into overdrive. I fully expect to hear Jackson's smug voice yell up at me at any moment.

Got you, princess.

But nothing comes, only more eerie silence coming from the abandoned carnival below.

I wait for the basket to stop swaying and try to push up once more, this time successfully getting into a sitting position without it moving.

I reach for the bar in the center and use it to steady myself, the electric pin pricks firing off in my leg as it wakes back up.

My voice of reason tells me not to look.

It's screaming for me to stay put and not test the limits any further.

I have to, though. I have to know for sure that he hasn't found me. I have to know whether I outsmarted my hunter, and that he is still out there scouring the grounds searching for me.

I grasp onto the side of the bucket, inching to the edge with such caution it's a wonder I'm moving at all.

My breath hitches in my throat and I close my eyes, trying to find the strength to look.

Don't do it.

I lean over the edge and exhale slowly, then open my eyes.

Jackson stands below me, head cocked to one side with a devious smirk playing on his lips. His eyes are swimming with victory and something darker.

I've been caught... *again*.

Chapter Nine

Jackson

I hold her stare as I lean over and turn the key. I keep the lights off, but the ride creaks as it slowly starts to spin.

She's out of her mind if she thinks I'm climbing up that thing. I looked everywhere I could think of, including *three* separate trash cans.

I didn't think she would scale an entire fucking Ferris wheel.

Those green eyes disappear from my sight, and I can only imagine what she's thinking.

"You almost did it!" I call out. "Really made me work for it this time!"

Now I'm going to make her repay the favor.

"Rule #3!" she calls back.

"Then you know what comes next!" I answer.

"You haven't caught me yet!" She's moving closer, only seven baskets away from me now.

Oh, I'm about to, princess.

"Nowhere else left for you to go. Turned out to be a shitty hiding place, hm?"

"Then why'd it take you so long to find me?"

"Who's to say I wasn't here the whole time? Maybe you're not as smart as you think you are."

No answer.

"How often are you *truly* the smartest person in the room?"

"I—"

"How much of that do we need to chalk up to delusion? I know what's-his-face was probably a fucking moron, but—wait, how many other guys have you said you've been with? Zero? I don't believe that."

"What?"

"I'm not calling you a slut but—yeah, I am. What's that saying? If it walks like a duck and talks like a duck?"

Five baskets away.

"Why are you here, Blair? I told you to go. I told you I didn't want you. Yet, you're still hanging around. You're nothing more than one of these miserable Southern belles, trying to prove something to yourself but only here as long as I don't get tired of you. What happens when I do?"

Four baskets.

"The game ends as soon as I get bored of your pussy. That's the only interesting thing about you, and I get bored easily, B." I hear the sound of her sniffling. "Poor me, the insecure girl who will let some stranger do whatever the fuck he wants with me as long as I get some attention."

Three baskets.

"What's your limit, huh? You gonna let me cut you up? Tie you up and leave you hanging? Beat you? Choke you until you pass out? Or does it not matter, as long as I keep my eyes on your face and my cock in your cunt? That's fucking pathetic. *You're* pathetic. And not worth my time. I could do much better than you. What about your friend? What was her name? *Mallory?* Yeah, why don't you call her? Bet she's a lot more fun. You're just a disgusting little freak."

Her basket is next. I wait until it comes around and hop over the edge to find her sitting in the corner of the basket, face streaked with tears and mascara. I crouch down, slipping my hand in her shorts.

"Look at you, wet and needy. I did nothing but tear you down the entire time, and you still want me. You ever get tired of being a whore?"

She looks up at me. "Jackson, you're scaring me."

I grin. "Punishments aren't supposed to be enjoyable, princess. Admit it, you like it anyway." I sit down on the seat, arms outstretched, legs taking up as much space as possible. "Which makes it not so much of a punishment, but it's still entertaining. Now come suck my cock."

"W-what?"

I pat my lap in response.

"You're kidding."

I lean forward slowly, dropping the smile from my face.

"Do I look like I'm kidding?"

She stares at me, as if she's waiting for me to say that this is all a joke. I tilt my head, waiting for her next move. She crawls forward, taking her time, until she reaches my lap. I lean back, watching her. She undoes my jeans with shaky hands, reaching in to pull my cock out. I'm already hard, and horny as hell. She stops, with one hand around me, squeezing gently.

"Now put it in your mouth."

She shoots me a look, then leans forward and wraps her lips around the tip. I grab the back of her head and push it down. My dick touches the back of her throat before she quickly lifts her head, gasping for air. My hand shoots out, grabbing her throat and bringing her close to me.

"You're *my* dirty little slut, princess. This isn't over yet. You just happen to be lucky that it's also your reward."

I move my hand to the back of her head again, gathering her hair and pushing her face down to my cock. She immediately opens her mouth, letting me glide over her tongue.

"Good girl. I knew you had it in you."

I groan from the feeling of her around me. She returns her hand to the base of my cock, squeezing firmly. Her teeth graze against me, and my head falls back as I moan. I push down on her head while moving my hips upward.

Fucking hell, it doesn't get much better than this.

She's getting into it now, bobbing up and down in time with her hand. We're almost to the top of the Ferris wheel, and I look out over the rest of the carnival. I wouldn't have met her if I didn't work here. What would I be doing instead? Stomping around, miserable as fuck, wishing for cold showers? I don't believe in fate, but this has gotta be close.

She hums, which brings me out of my thoughts. Her other hand moves to my balls, massaging them, and that heat deep in my stomach is getting more intense.

"Fuck, Blair. You're doing so well," I moan, which eggs her on. She increases the pace, and this has to be one of the best blowjobs I've ever gotten. "I'm about to—"

She deep throats me and gags before she quickly learns to relax and breathe through her nose. She moves her head back and forth, moaning. The vibrations have me shooting down her throat. I'm seeing fucking stars.

What the hell was that?

Blair licks her way up my cock, then sits back on her heels, sucking her bottom lip into her mouth. Once I gather myself, I lean forward, pressing my lips against hers.

"My perfect little slut," I tell her. Her eyes gleam as she grins. I kiss her again before licking up the tears still running down her cheeks.

We're only a couple baskets away from the ground, so I tuck myself back in my jeans and hop out, turning the key to *OFF.* I return to our basket and help her climb out, brushing her hair behind her ear. She looks up at me, mischief twinkling in her eyes. I hold her face and run my thumb along her lips.

"Tell me about the worst thing that's ever happened to you."

Chapter Ten

Blair

"Besides tonight?"

Jackson narrows his eyes and takes a warning step toward me. "Blair."

What the fuck is going on? Now he wants to talk?

"I'm sorry, but you have to give me some grace here Jackson. A few minutes ago you were saying horrible things to me and treating me like some cheap whore, now you're casually trying to get to know me?"

He shifts. "I'm failing to see your point. Are you not a cheap whore?"

My jaw drops open, not one bit of this making a lick of sense.

"Close your mouth, B. And stop looking at me like I'm speaking a different language."

"A different language might make more sense. Your multiple personalities are giving me whiplash!" I throw my hands up and lean against the cold metal railing.

One side of Jackson's mouth turns upward into a boyish grin. "Is that so?"

"Yes, yes it is. I know absolutely nothing about you, other than your penchant for turning schoolyard games into something deeply disturbing. One second you're making me experience more pleasure than I could have ever imagined, and in the next you're making me question every single fucking thing about myself." I cross my arms and let out a deep sigh. "A few hours ago I was Blair, a girl who never took risks and had only ever given my body to one person. A person I'd dated for years. And now I'm running through a dirty carnival being chased by a man who wants to punish me, and liking it. You're reading me like a book and instead of using that to—I don't know—be nice to me, you're breaking me down."

My mind races as I start to really think about what has happened tonight and what I've done. My mouth goes dry and a tightness fills my chest, the world around me suddenly feeling like it's running out of air.

"So let's get to know one another," Jackson says in a soft voice, taking a step toward me. "You answer my questions and I'll answer yours."

I look up at him through my lashes, his closeness bringing a strange sense of comfort that I can't explain.

"A game within a game," Jackson laughs, the first time I think I've heard a real laugh come from him. "Like Saw."

"Huh?"

His brow shoots up. "You know, Saw. A game within a game?"

I shake my head slowly, no idea what the hell he is talking about.

"You've got to be fucking kidding me. Jigsaw? Puppet on a tricycle?"

"Is that a friend of yours or something?"

He looks appalled at my lack of understanding for whatever weird reference he's making.

"Oh, Blair. So many things I would teach you if I had the time." His hand rests on the side of my cheek. "Forget it. Back to the questions. Do we have a deal?"

I nod, and he joins me at my side.

"The worst thing that has ever happened to me was losing my twin sister," I say, my voice barely a whisper. "She died when I was twelve, and I don't think there will ever be any pain that can hurt more than that."

"What happened?"

Flashbacks play in my mind, distorted and hazy like an old home movie. "She was sick. There was something wrong with her heart. She was on the transplant list, but the call never came. Then one day she was just gone. She was my best friend. My other half."

That feeling rises to my throat. The one where it burns and hurts to swallow. It always happens when I try not to cry.

"I killed my best friend," Jackson says nonchalantly, without a trace of emotion in his voice.

I try to convince myself that I'm hearing things. That whatever I just heard couldn't possibly be what he meant.

"I didn't mean to, but I did it."

I can't speak, the words are trapped inside me.

"I don't even remember what we were arguing about. That's what makes it so fucked up. Every other detail is imprinted in my mind. All except that." He twists his fingers together, fidgeting, the conversation obviously uncomfortable for him to talk about with me. "He shoved me, and I hit him. He fell back, but then came at me harder. I've never been able to control my anger, always quick to use my fists to solve my problems. We were at a party and everyone around us laughed about it at first. It wasn't the first time we'd roughed each other up over something stupid."

I look out at the darkness in front of us, unable to look at him. Jackson was unlike any other man I'd ever met, but deep down I truly never thought my life was in real danger.

But now?

"When we didn't let up after a few blows you could feel the energy shift. People around us stopped laughing and started yelling. Started telling us to stop. We didn't stop, though. He landed a right hook and I almost went down, but I managed to stay on my feet somehow. I swung again, my fist hitting his temple. He fell straight back like a domino and his head slammed into the base of the fireplace."

Bile rises in my throat as I listen to his story.

"I remember the screams, the blood, and the look on every single fucking person's face. They didn't look at me like I was Jackson anymore. No, they looked at me and saw a monster. Fuck, I guess that does sort of make me a monster. I did three years for manslaughter. It probably should have been more, but I took a deal. When I got out, I left town and never looked back." He sighs. "It is what it is."

I stand there, unable to meet his gaze even though I can feel his stare on me. He waits for me to say something, anything to give away what is going through my mind after his admission.

There have been more than a few times that Jackson has scared me tonight, but deep in the recesses of my psyche I never truly believed I was in danger.

Until now.

This man had taken a life. The life of someone he loved.

And me?

I'm just some girl he barely knows.

"Are you afraid of me now, princess?" he asks, voice low.

"I was already afraid of you," I answer, folding my arms in front of me.

He moves so that he's directly in front of me, blocking my field of vision. I look down, unable to meet his obsidian gaze.

"That's what makes our little game so much fun." His voice is smooth, unnaturally smooth considering the conversation we're having. "If you weren't afraid, this wouldn't be nearly as enjoyable as it is."

"Why do you want me to be scared of you, Jackson?"

I'm trying to understand him, trying to figure out why seeing the blood drain from my face when I know I've got nowhere to run gets him off.

Even worse, I'm trying to understand why I agreed to it in the first place.

His hand cups my chin and tilts it up, forcing me to look at him.

"Aren't pretty girls supposed to be scared of monsters?"

What if I'm more afraid of myself and the lines that I didn't even know I was willing to cross. Tonight has shown me that maybe I'm not the girl who wants to run away from the monster, but maybe the one who secretly wants to be found by him.

"How does this end?" I ask, letting out the breath I was holding.

He looks up at the sky and then back at me. "You're free when the sun comes up, Blair. Until then, you belong to me."

I gulp, trying to ignore the thrumming between my legs at his possessiveness.

"That leads me to something else. We need a safe word. I've held back as long as I can, but now I want to see just how far we can take this."

I can't help the nervous giggle that escapes my lips. "You call that holding back?"

Jackson frowns. "Princess, I can promise you I've held back. The things I want to do to you..." He trails off, his mind seemingly going through a slideshow of all the depravity he wants to unleash on me. "In order for me to do those things I need you to understand that while I am in control, you still have power."

"A safe word," I repeat, my mind racing through all the possible things that would require one.

"Yes, it can be whatever you want. Just know, when you say it, *everything* stops."

"Are you going to hurt me?" I ask.

Something dark shimmers in his eyes and it sends a chill over my body.

"Yes," he replies, offering me a sickly sweet smile.

I should run.

Not run and hide like before, just run. Run to my car and get the fuck out of here before I go too far.

Every single shred of logic within me is screaming that I need to get as far away from this man as humanly possible.

But then there is a new voice, whispering, *"You won't run. You can't. You want this. You want him to hurt you, and you're going to like it."*

I grab a strand of hair and twist it between my fingertips, a nervous habit I've had for as long as I can remember.

"The safe word?" he asks again, and I take my bottom lip into my mouth.

"I don't know, just any word?"

"Whatever you want."

I look around me, trying to think of something. It seems only fitting that I choose something that matches the setting.

There is a ticket booth close by, a few trash cans, and a row of portable toilets.

None of that seems appropriate.

I look behind us and see a large, covered arena. The moonlight gives me just enough to make out what is inside.

"Bumper cars?" I say, uncertainty evident in my tone.

"Not what I was expecting, but I can work with that." He takes a few steps back and extends an arm. "Now that we both understand how this is going to work, I want you to run. And while you run I want you to think about all the deliciously horrible things I'm going to do to you when I find you."

"But—" I begin, but he places his finger over his lips and lets out a whispered *shh* sound.

"I'm not going to tell you again, Blair. I don't like repeating myself."

Chapter Eleven

Jackson

"Go," I tell her as I turn around and start counting. She immediately starts running; no hesitation this time.

I've been pretty gentle with her up until now, testing the limits of what she can take. I didn't want to scare her away too soon, but now all bets are off. I'm going to make her worst nightmares come to life.

Let's see what she really looks like under that front she puts up.

Luring people into cages should be harder than it actually is. Apparently, all it takes these days is a phone. People can't *live* without their phones. So when Blair left hers behind, I knew I had the perfect bait. Especially since she walks around without a password on the thing. It's like she wants it to be stolen.

Now I'm in the haunted fun house, waiting for her to "hide" in here.

I learned my lesson at the Ferris wheel. She hasn't really left my sight since. I gave chase, like I knew she wanted, cutting her off at different places I knew she would go, herding her like a sheep.

It's dark in here, the shadows camouflaging me easily. The dry ice machines are still going, covering the floor in a dense fog. There's four cages here—ranging in size—that are usually locked so no one tries to climb in. Three of them are still closed. The smallest one "coincidentally" has the door hanging open. She'll fit, but just barely.

I hear a small crash and her whisper-shouting, "Ouch!" She's hopping on one foot, her hands rubbing her shin. She kicks the box she ran into once she's back on both feet.

I round the corner while dialing her number and lowering the mask I found, keeping my footsteps silent.

Blair runs toward the sound of her phone. "What the hell? I've been looking everywhere for this!"

She disappears into the fog. When I see her again, she's halfway inside the cage, arm outstretched. I'm almost right on top of her. She really needs to be more observant.

She groans, her fingers barely brushing against the phone.

Come on. A little more.

She inches forward, squeezing herself through the cage door, and grabs the phone. It rings two more times before she finally accepts the call and puts the phone to her ear.

"Mallory?"

"Not quite."

I slam the door closed, the locking mechanism sliding into place. She immediately starts panicking, dropping the phone and wrapping her fingers against the bars of the cage. I walk around to the back of the cage, and crouch down to her level. She's stuck in the same position, on her hands and knees. She already has tears in her eyes.

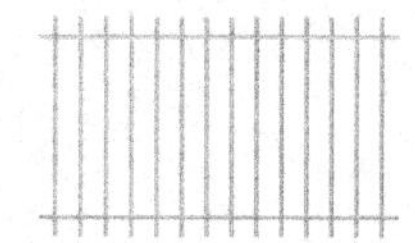

"No! Not this! Let me out!" she screams.

"Can't do that, little freak. We made a deal, remember?"

"I can't breathe!" she wails.

I gesture to the open bars. "Yes, you can."

Blair presses her face against the bars. Her chest is moving rapidly, and she's gasping for air. She's about to send herself into a full-blown panic attack.

Is she fucking claustrophobic?

I can't help the small grin that creeps across my face.

I look around, my eyes landing on a wooden plank to my right. Reaching over to grab it, I look back at the bars. Yeah, this will fit. Standing, I walk back to the front of the cage and use the plank to smack her ass, making Blair jolt forward.

"Fuck! What was that?" she screeches, turning her head to look at me.

I wave the wooden plank. "I had to shut you up somehow."

"That was unnecessary."

"It worked, didn't it? You're not panicking anymore." I look down at her and notice her pussy glistening. "And you're wet."

"No, I'm not."

I smack her ass again. "Then what's dripping down your thighs right now?"

"You're brutal," she groans.

"Stop trying to hide yourself from me."

"I'm hiding? What's up with the mask?"

I tap on the red clown nose. "I'm Shifty! Isn't this fun?"

"You're insane."

I take the mask off, and drop it into the cage.

She's positioned perfectly for me, and I need to finish what I started here. Standing, I open the cage door. I hear her sigh of relief as the hinges creak. She starts to move backwards, but I press the plank against her.

"Where do you think you're going?" I ask.

"You're not letting me go?"

I can see her breathing quicken again. She scares too easily. This is nothing. What's a little tight space against the rest of the world? Or me?

"Tell me, what's scarier? This cage or me?"

She gives me a look, like *this is not the time*. I disagree.

"I'm gonna need you to respond," I probe.

"The cage."

"That was the wrong answer."

"Fine. You."

"Well, now it's not genuine." I frown while shoving her shorts down, leaving them to pool at her knees. Goddamn claustrophobia.

She may not be into the mask, but I think it's kind of hot. Especially with her semi-naked.

"Put the mask on. You're not getting out of this cage, so you're going to have to get through it."

"How does the mask help?"

"Oh, it doesn't," I lie. "Put it on."

Her breathing will be louder while she's wearing the mask. It'll make her more conscious of the breaths she takes, like a breathing exercise. And if she starts freaking out again, I'll be able to notice it faster.

She slips the mask over her face. I run the wood over the globe of her ass before smacking it again, making her yelp. I alternate between spanking her with the plank and kneading her angry skin with my hand.

We quickly settle into a routine her body is getting used to. She flinches a second before the plank comes down on her ass, and her squeals are turning more into moans. I'm not giving her enough time to think about the tight space she's in, and I'm shocking her body just enough to keep her breathing consistent.

I run a finger down her ass to her pussy, coating it in her wetness. I circle her entrance before slipping it inside her. She releases a breath, and rocks back into my hand. I return with another finger, then another, stretching her out. She moves from her hands to her forearms, ripping off the mask, and rewards me with those breathy moans I love. My cock jerks slightly at the sound of her pleasure. It wants more pain.

I remove my fingers from her, and smack her pussy with the wooden board. She's startled so much she screams, and bangs her head against the top of the cage. I laugh, and give her another spank.

"Too much? Is my desperate, needy slut reaching her limit?" I taunt. I plunge my fingers back inside of her, her body undulating with the waves of pain and pleasure I'm offering her. "Answer me." I punish her by pressing the plank flush against her pussy, allowing her to ride it until the brink of the edge before pulling her back.

"I-I... fuck," she moans. "I... want..."

"You want what? Spit it out, princess. I'm not doing shit until you use your words."

She looks back at me. Those tears are still running down her cheeks. She's blubbering, shaking uncontrollably, and a huge fucking mess. All the remaining blood in my body rushes to my dick. She's perfect. I'm rock hard.

"Use me."

Fuuuuuuck.

The sound coming from deep in my chest right now isn't normal. I'm going to wreck her; fucking ruin her. She's not walking out of tonight completely whole. I'm keeping a piece for myself. I'll take it right after I break her wide open.

I pull my cock out, dropping to my knees behind her. Drops of pre-cum dribble down my shaft. I hone in on the sight before me—Blair on her hands and knees, ass up and face down, willing to give whatever I want from her. Her ass and thighs are mottled red from my punishing blows, and all I can think about is how I want more. I want her to bleed for me.

I line myself up and sink inside her, giving her no time to adjust before I'm withdrawing and driving back into her, over and over, harsh and fast. Her cries and whimpers match my groans, both of us getting louder as I pound her pussy. I suck a finger into my mouth before pressing it against her hole. She immediately tenses up.

"Trust me," I soothe. "I got you."

She moans and relaxes enough for me to breach the tight ring of muscle. I move my finger slowly, but in time with my thrusts.

"Oh, God," she groans.

"Just me, princess. Just me."

Her body starts to loosen up, accepting me more. She meets my thrusts, sweat gliding down her body. I snake my other hand between her legs, rubbing her clit in slow circles.

"Please—"

"Come on, B. You know you want to let go." My thrusts pick up until I'm rutting into her violently, punishing her clit with my fingers, and plugging her ass. She cries out, her lower half moving on its own accord until she can't hold it anymore. Tossing her head back, she comes apart as I devastate her body.

I continue my assault, making sure I draw out every whine I'm due until my hips stagger and I'm falling right behind her.

"That's right. Drain me dry, you dirty slut."

She collapses onto the floor, turning onto her back, chest heaving. I allow her to catch her breath, picking my new friend back up and thumbing its sharp edges.

I'm not even close to done yet.

"You like being chased? After that, I'm feeling generous. One more chance. I'll let you out since you've been such a good girl for me... but if I catch you this time, I'm not stopping until I've had my fill of you. And I'm fucking ravenous, Blair."

She visibly gulps, terror strewn all over her face. "What... what does that mean?" she whispers.

"You better remember your safe word. 'No' means nothing to me. 'Stop' means go." I get real close to her face, my breath fanning across her lips. "All that matters is what I want."

"The safe word is bumper cars."

"Those are actually safe *words*, but good job."

"Huh?"

"Safe words. As in, two words. Really proving my 'smartest person in the room' point."

"Stop being so damn mean!"

"I am not a nice person. I don't where you got that insane idea from."

"No shit."

I grin, standing and pulling up my jeans. I open the cage, and watch her crawl out slowly. I tap the wooden plank against my foot, looking over her as she moves past me. As soon as she clears the cage door, she rocks back on her knees and sighs in relief.

"Did I cure your claustrophobia?" I ask.

She shoots me a look. "Not even close."

She moves to stand, but I place the wood on top of her head. "No standing."

"What?" she squeaks.

"'*No shit'*? Really? You thought you were going to get away with that? You can fucking crawl."

Chapter Twelve

Blair

"That's right. Crawl for me, Blair. Crawl like the pathetic little slut you are."

You would think being completely debased by this man would be doing a number on my self-esteem. That it would be causing some sort of existential crisis where I second-guess every single thing about myself for enjoying it, but it's having the opposite effect. Sure, in the beginning maybe. But now? Being broken down and seeing my pieces strewn out over the dirty floor is one of the most liberating things I've ever experienced.

There is no place here for perfect Blair.

No, here that version of myself is so far out of reach her edges have gone fuzzy.

This Blair, the one who is crawling on her hands and knees across splintered wood while her hunter closes in, is the only version that makes sense.

I'm not sure how to explain it, or that I even could if given the opportunity. It doesn't fucking matter anyway. I don't recognize myself anymore.

I can feel the skin on my knees and palms ripping, but the pain is pushed so far back into the recesses of my mind I barely register it. All I can focus on is my pounding heart and the fire-hot blood pumping furiously in my veins.

I crawl until the crown of my head slams into one of the walls.

I let out a strained hiss and rub at the place where a massive knot is already beginning to reveal itself.

"Gotta be more careful, princess. That sounded like it hurt." Jackson's taunting voice echoes through the narrow passageway.

This time isn't like the others. He is too close, and there's no where to fucking run.

I try to get up to my feet, using the molding that sits halfway up the wall to lift my weight. My arms feel like jello, shaking uncontrollably as I pull up. Bracing myself against the wall I try to take a deep breath, needing to get my adrenaline in check before my heart quite literally explodes.

I blink rapidly, trying to force my eyes to adjust to the darkness around me.

There is no way out.

No place to hide.

A faux window with tattered curtains is centered on a small wall.

It's a terrible idea, but at this point there is no other option.

I try to keep my footsteps as quiet as possible, not even flinching when my toe catches on an exposed nail.

My hands fumble against the fabric, shoving it to the side so I can slink behind it. The first layer is sheer, but a thick red material makes up the second. It is long enough to cover my feet, and maybe... just maybe the lack of lighting will camouflage me.

I hold my breath, wondering if he can hear my heart slamming into my chest. If he can hear the sweat dripping from my brow and hitting collarbone.

Jackson's tongue clicks as he rounds the corner and my mouth goes dry.

"Silly girl," he calls out, voice oozing confidence. "You've run into a dead end."

I freeze in place, not daring to move. Not even the slightest twinge.

I can hear his fingers trailing against the wall, slowly.

"Even in the dark I know every square inch of this place," he continues, taunting me with each step closer. "I can *feel* when something is out of place."

A confusing mixture of fear and excitement fills me. Fear over what he will do to me this time, and excitement because I know deep down whatever it is will bring me pleasure.

It's so fucked up. It's almost too much.

The sound of his footsteps stop right in front of me, and I swear I can feel the heat from his breath on my cheeks.

"Come out to play, princess."

I don't move, refusing to admit defeat so easily.

"Don't make me drag you."

It's a threat that terrifies me, but I don't give in.

His large hands gather the fabric of the curtains and pull them to each side, revealing me to him. He leans in so that his nose grazes mine, a surprisingly soft gesture for him. I am not dense enough to think the softness will continue.

"Boo," he whispers, and my pussy is drenched.

With alarming speed he grasps a fistful of my hair at the scalp and wretches my head to one side. His feet are moving and it takes every ounce of strength and balance I can muster to stop from tripping over my own as he pulls me down the hallway.

I cry out, but he only laughs.

His grip on me by only my hair is so tight tears begin to brim at my eyes.

I lose my footing and my hip slams into the hard floor beneath me. I have no clue how the wad of hair in his fist hasn't ripped out at the root.

I almost gag from the pain.

Jackson kneels down to face me, his free hand cupping my cheek and brushing away a fallen tear.

"Do you want me to let go, Blair?"

I know better than to ask for that. He made it very clear that the only way I was stopping this was my safe word, but that meant *truly* stopping it.

I wasn't ready for my night with him to be over.

I shake my head, another tear escaping my traitorous eyes.

"That's my good girl," he praises, fingers wrapping around my cheeks and squeezing hard. "You take what I give you and you like it." He licks my lips. "You want me to slow down? I'd love to hear you beg some more. Your words are so pretty. Do you like begging?"

"Y-yes." I force the word out of my mouth and he rewards me with a smile.

I would do just about anything to see that smile. To see that something I have done has pleased him. Even if it means betraying myself.

He stands, tightening his hold on my hair, and begins to drag me further into the house. I clasp my hands around his wrist, desperate for some sort of leverage to make it more bearable. We reach a familiar large room. It's the one with the mirrors.

How did we get back here?

Jackson pulls me to the center and releases me, my body landing with a thud against the wooden floor.

He takes a slow lap around the perimeter of the room, his eyes taking in all the things around us. He focuses back on me, his gaze starting at my face then trailing down my body until stopping between my legs.

"Look how wet you are, Blair. You look fucking delicious." The words seep out of his mouth and wrap around me. "Such a needy little whore."

I sit up and wrap my arms around my knees, cradling myself.

"Don't you dare hide your body from me," Jackson grits out through clenched teeth. "Take your shirt off."

I hesitate, not wanting to remove the very last stitch of clothing that remains on my body. He's already taken everything else. I have nothing left.

"It wasn't a request, Blair. Now."

I slowly release my knees and grab the hem of my t-shirt. I pull it over my head, tossing it to the side. My instinct is to cover myself again with my arms, but I fight the urge.

He crosses the room and uses his boot to force my legs open. Air hits my exposed pussy and sends a shiver down my spine.

"Please, Jackson," I whine, begging him. For what, I don't know.

I hate that he's right. I am acting like a needy little whore.

Why am I acting like this?

"Tsk-tsk-tsk," he chides. "Tell me no, Blair. Tell me to stop. That you don't want this."

He takes a step back, admiring my naked body. His tongue glides over the edges of his teeth, and my skin pricks in anticipation.

I can't do that. I do want this. Don't I?

Isn't this what you've been asking for all night?

He shakes his head, chuckling. "I want you to take me in your throat again." His fingers expertly work at the belt and buttons on his jeans. "That show you put on when we were on the Ferris wheel isn't one I'll be able to forget any time soon."

I sit up, eyes wide as he removes his hard length and fists it.

His steps toward me are slow, and when I can reach out and touch him I move to sit up on my knees.

Before I can even speak he slides himself into my mouth. He pushes deeper, not phased by my gags. I swirl my tongue around him, trying to focus on breathing out of my nose as he thrusts in and out.

His large hands grasp onto each side of my face, holding me firmly in place as he moves. My hands find the back of his thighs, needing something to grab onto. My nails dig into the thick material of his jeans and I wish they were gone. I want to feel his skin.

"Princess, I am going to coat your throat. I want you to swallow." He grunts in between thrusts. "Every. Single. Drop."

I know he's close when he buries himself in me, my lips meeting the base.

His release fills my throat like an explosion and I struggle to keep it all down. I choke against him, but he doesn't release me until he's felt my throat bob against him.

He pulls out of me and I fall forward, barely catching myself before I hit the floor.

"Get up," he demands, and I try.

His palm wraps around my wrist and yanks me upward, obviously not having the patience to wait for me to do it myself. He's already hard again, though I'm not really sure how.

He shoves me toward the wall of mirrors, my body colliding with the glass. Shards shatter against the ground, and when he presses my face against it I wince.

Warm liquid drips from my cheek and I know it's cut me.

"Wait—"

His hand wraps around my throat, cutting me off, and my back automatically arches for him.

I place my palms against the mirrored wall, my fingers slicing against the cracks.

"I don't know that I'll ever get enough of you, Blair," he rasps against the back of my neck. "For once in my life, I may need more than just one night."

My chest swells at his admission but I'm almost scared to acknowledge it. It doesn't seem like something Jackson would ever admit out loud, and I don't know if my pride could take it if he took it back. I need more. I don't want this to be it.

"Jackson, wait—" I try again.

His free hand glides down my back and rests on the curve of my ass. His palm cracks against my skin, slapping my right cheek hard.

"Fuck, this is all mine," he growls.

He slaps my ass again, making me jolt forward into the mirror. I can feel the glass digging into me with every movement I make.

"Stop," I beg, swallowing hard. "I can't."

I don't have to see his eyes to know they are dark and hungry, desire dancing in them.

Without so much as a warning he thrusts inside me, positioning my hips so I can take him completely.

I gasp at the fullness, my head leaning back in ecstasy as he buries himself inside me.

He pulls out and drives back in with no holding back, slamming me into the mirrors with each pump. I can't control my moans; they come out loud and wild.

The hand around my throat tightens and tiny lights swirl across my vision.

"That's right, you fucking whore. You take it so—" he groans in between thrusts. "—well."

My fingers slide over a loose shard on the wall, and when my hand wraps around it, it pulls away with ease. My grasp tightens over the shard, the pain from the sharp edges feeling odd but good as it digs into my skin.

I can feel every ridge of his length as it slams into the walls of my pussy, my clit thrumming with hunger.

I don't realize what I've done until I hear Jackson growl my name.

"Blair."

I can faintly make out our reflection in the hazy mirror, and what I see doesn't seem real.

The glass shard is pressed to his throat, red liquid beaded around where the tip meets his skin. He's slamming into me, not giving a fuck that his life is quite literally in my hands.

Fuck, this is so wrong.

"Do it," he murmurs.

I press the tip down harder against him, reveling when his eyes squeeze shut.

I can barely hear anything around me anymore, rolling waves of heat crashing over me with such intensity I can barely stand.

Jackson groans again as I tighten around him, my climax building fast.

"Come for me, my beautiful little freak."

He thrusts in again, so deep that I don't think I've ever felt anything come so close to piercing my core.

Wetness spills out of me as the orgasm tears through my body.

I look at the reflection again. The trail of blood dripping down his neck, the shard of glass in my hand, and the scrapes and cuts that mar my skin.

Another tidal wave of fear slams into me.

Not over what I'd done, no. The fear was that now I had crossed some invisible line in the sand that I would never be able to come back from.

Am I too far gone?

Chapter Thirteen

Jackson

"Fuck, princess, you're something else," I say as I nuzzle my nose against the back of her neck, inhaling. Somehow she still smells like lavender.

Instead of a response, I feel Blair's body tense up. She drops the shard of glass as her eyes meet mine in the mirror's reflection.

"I'm sorry," she whispers.

"Sorry?" I ask. "For what?"

"I hurt you. I-I don't know what happened. I just—and then—"

"What the fuck are you going on about?"

"I—you—" she sobs.

What the fuck is wrong with her?

"What? This?" I swipe my hand across the side of my throat and lick my palm before holding it up for her to see. "This is nothing. Look at you." I point to her right cheek. "That's gonna scar."

Blair presses her fingertips against the jagged cut slicing across her face. "Fuck," she whimpers, tears running freely.

"Don't worry, you're still hot." I pull away from her, shoving my half-hard dick back inside my jeans.

She sniffles, swiping at her nose. "You don't have to be an ass all the time! This is serious!"

"Oh, what? You realize you're not the goody two-shoes you thought you were? You got a little carried away and now you're seeing a version of yourself you don't like and you're fucking everything up."

"I'm fucking everything up? You're the psycho carnie that's been chasing me around all night!"

"I think you're just as psycho as me. Only problem is that I'm not standing here lying to myself about it. You liked every single part of tonight. Even when you *did* finally tell me no. You still wanted it all."

"Fuck you!"

"Stop trying to make me the fucking villain here, Blair. You chose not to use your safe words. Admit it. Deep down inside that tight little body of yours is a fucked up, sadomasochistic whore that's just rearing to be let out of her cage. You just wanted me to force you across the finish line."

"I am not like that."

"Yes, you are. And I just proved it while making you come around my cock."

"No, you didn't."

"Do you need me to do it again? We've literally been doing it all night."

"Why are you like this? I swear, you're the most frustrating person I know."

"So are you! Blair, the more you talk, the softer I get. Please shut the fuck up."

Her eyes narrow before she stomps off.

"I said please!" I shout after her, throwing my hands up.

Jesus, what is it with her?

I should cut her loose now, before we both get in too deep. It's not too late. I think.

She'll stop and come back.

Right?

Why is she not stopping?

I run after her, and grab her wrist. "Where the fuck are you going?"

"Away from you." She tries to wrench away from me to no avail, so she starts hitting me. "Let go!"

"Blair." She's lost it, flailing around like a child. "Blair—" I repeat, grabbing both of her wrists. I hold them against my chest. She looks up at me, daggers in her eyes, before kicking me right in the shin. "Fucking bi—" I don't get to finish my sentence before she decides to kick me in the balls. I drop immediately, groaning.

I'm starting to regret this whole "show her how to be someone else" idea I had.

I'm bent over, cupping my crotch, cursing up a storm when I turn my head to the side and catch a glimpse of her. I look up to see her trying to stifle a giggle.

"Oh, is that funny?"

She bursts out in laughter—it racks through her whole body and she bends over gasping for air in between guffaws.

"Alright, fine. Maybe I deserved it. But remember that when you're begging for mercy." I move to stand quickly, throwing her over my shoulder and smacking her ass. She squeals, but doesn't put up much of a fight. Maybe I played right into her devilish little hands.

I'm starting to wonder who really has the upper hand here.

I let my hand creep up the back of her thigh as I walk. I hear her sigh as I squeeze her ass, then slide my fingers right against her pussy. She's slick, just like she's been all night. I bring two of my fingers to my mouth, tasting her. God, I can't fucking get enough.

I can feel her grab onto the back of my shirt when I slide those same fingers into her pussy. She bucks, and I grab her ankle to keep her from sliding off of me.

"Jackson..." she murmurs as I fuck her.

I keep walking, seeing my trailer get closer and closer. She starts squirming, squeezing her thighs around my hand. I band my arm around both of her legs, keeping her still as I pick up the pace. She let a moan slip, and uses my shirt as a makeshift gag.

She's getting close, clamping around me when I curl my fingers.

I start to hear birds chirp in the distance. Fuck.

I stop, and let her down slowly. As her body trails down mine, she wraps her legs around my waist. I grip her thighs and smash my mouth against hers. She opens up for me, allowing full access. We're a tangle of tongues and teeth, no finesse as we try to devour each other. I nip her bottom lip and she gasps, grinding herself against my erection.

It's a race against the dawn at this point, and I think we both know that. I move my lips to her throat as she runs her hands through my hair, tilting her head back. My trailer is only a few feet away, but I need her right fucking now. I drop to my knees, laying her on her back in the dirt. It's perfect really, since this has to be a quick and dirty fuck.

I unzip my jeans, my cock springing out immediately. I take it in my hand, spitting on it before lining myself against her entrance. She's looking at me in anticipation, biting her lip. I lift my shirt off of me, balling it up.

"Open," I tell her. She complies, and I stuff my shirt in her mouth. I stroke my cock twice before thrusting into her, bottoming out. She arches her back, screams muffled. Fuck, I'm glad I did that before she woke everyone up.

I remove myself from her almost entirely before driving back into her. I lower my head to tease her nipple with my mouth, sucking and biting, before moving to the other one.

Fuck, I'm going to miss these tits. This pussy. The way she looks at me.

Her.

Her hands are in my hair again, pulling my strands as I pump in and out of her. She's mumbling incoherently around the gag, as I work her nipples with my tongue. I remove her hands from my hair and pin them to the ground.

"You're so fucking perfect for me. I wish I could hear you scream my name, princess."

I remove my shirt from her mouth, replacing it with my fingers. She sucks on them like the good girl she is. Heat pools low in my stomach at the sight of her. Hair splayed around her head, eyes glazed over, mouth slightly open. Careless.

"I need you like this all the time. You look so pretty when you're being fucked senseless." I drag my pelvis against hers as I fuck her, attempting for as much friction between our bodies as possible. Peppering kisses up her chest, I bury my head in her neck, sucking and biting there as well. I need to leave as much of me on her as I can. She's getting close to the edge again, her breaths coming in a heavy staccato. Blair writhes under me as her eyes roll to the back of her head. "I fucking love the way you break for me, Blair. I could watch you come over and over again. For hours."

I tilt my hips, trying to get as deep as possible. We both smell like sweat and dirt, but the only thing I care about is her pleasure.

"My filthy little slut. Stop being scared of yourself. Say you're mine. Tell me I can keep you."

"I'm yours," she whimpers as I wrap my fingers around her throat, her nails scraping down my back.

"Come for me, princess," I say as I cover her lips with mine. I swallow her moans as she comes around my cock, long and deep, for what seems like forever. I thrust once more before I'm coming, her pussy squeezing my cock.

Reality crashes back in hard when I realize there's a blue haze surrounding us. Dawn's caught up to us, and that means the game is over.

I look down at Blair, brushing away her hair from her face. Her eyes are holding onto some emotion I don't know the name of, but I know it's not good. I pull away from her, helping her sit up. We stand and silently make our way the last few feet to my trailer. I pull out my keys and unlock the door, letting her enter first. She's covered in dirt, blood, and sweat. So am I. I desperately need a shower, but first, the hard part.

She looks around my trailer, chewing on her lip, before turning to me.

"Game's over," she says.

"Yeah. You can go back to your perfect life now."

She fidgets, shifting her weight back and forth between her feet.

"Are you okay? Can I get you anything? Water or something?" I ask.

"Um..." She gestures to her naked body. "Something to cover up with?"

"Oh shit, yeah." I walk to the bedroom, searching for a clean shirt. All I come up with is some old sweatshirt. I return, offering it to her. She takes it, immediately putting it on. I already hate this. I want her naked all the time.

I need to get it together. Another night, another girl. That's it. That's fine.

It's fine. I'm fine.

"Thanks," she says. "Maybe I'll see you around?"

"Sure," I lie.

I'm not expecting to see her after she walks out of here. It'll be like this never happened.

Fucking do something, Jackson. What happened to "tell me I can keep you"?

It was just sex.

God, I wanna keep her so bad.

I'm frozen. I must look like a deer in headlights. She probably thinks I'm horrible.

Stop being like this. Am I broken? Did she fucking break me?

She moves past me while I'm stuck in place.

I can't watch her leave or else I'll do something crazy.

She opens the door, hesitating.

Don't look. Don't look.

Then she sighs and leaves.

Maybe calling her a cheap whore was a little much.

Chapter Fourteen

Blair

The drive home is an out of body experience. It's like my focus is on the road, but somehow I'm so far removed from reality it doesn't seem like I am the one with my hands on the wheel.

I grip the leather tightly, trying to regain some semblance of normalcy.

My bare legs feel strange against the seats, and with nothing but the sound of tires spinning against the asphalt to drown out my thoughts I slip further away from the present.

I'll show you what it feels like to be bad,

The things I did were bad.

That's right, beg for it.

I had begged for it. Over and over and over again.

My perfect little slut.

His voice echoes in my mind on a torturous loop. I'm stuck on the merry-go-round and I can't fucking get off.

Aren't pretty girls supposed to be scared of monsters?

I *am* scared. I'm fucking terrified. Terrified of the monster I let in my mouth, in between my legs, and into my mind.

I'm even more afraid of the marks he's left on me. Not the ones you can see. No, those will fade away with time. The ones that have me knotted up with fear are the ones you can't see. The marks that I can *feel*.

I don't know that I'll ever get my fill of you, Blair.

That's good, Jackson, because I don't know if I'll ever be able to go back to the girl I was before stepping foot inside that fucking carnival. He's ruined me. Broken me so that nothing *normal* will ever feel right again.

Tiny fragments of me are scattered across that place, just like the shards of glass that cover the floor of the fun house.

I pull into the parking spot directly in front of my building, the sky still that beautiful blend of pinks and oranges that come with the sunrise.

The soles of my feet feel numb, and I barely notice the sensation of loose rocks against them as I make my way to the stairs.

I am operating on autopilot.

Two flights up, turn right, slide the key in the lock. Twist the knob, step inside.

Flip on the lights and breathe.

Nothing feels the same anymore.

My apartment is too quiet, the walls are too white, and the person looking back at me in the reflection of my bathroom mirror doesn't look like me.

Her skin is dirty and covered in dried blood.

Our blood.

Her hair hangs in a tangled mess over her shoulders, and a newfound darkness swirls in her eyes like black ink dropped into a pool of blue water.

"Who are you?" I ask the stranger, and when our mouths move in unison my breath hitches in my throat.

Jackson's sweatshirt swallows my frame, and when I wrap my arms around myself I can smell him all over me.

The shower calls my name but for some reason I'm in no hurry to wash away my sins. Instead I stare at them for a little while longer.

"What the hell happened to you?" Mallory exclaims when she takes in my appearance.

Full coverage foundation helps, but the very visible mark on my face from the glass is basically impossible to hide. Especially from the laser focused gaze of my best friend.

She takes my cheeks in her palms and pulls my face closer so she can examine the wound.

"It was that fucking carnie, wasn't it?" Her breath is hot against my skin and I pull away.

"No, Mal. It wasn't."

I should have put a tiny bit of effort into coming up with some sort of cover story, but unfortunately my brain has been the consistency of scrambled eggs since I left the carnival.

"I have known you for too long, B. I can tell when you're lying. You're fucking terrible at it, anyway."

I take a sip from the latte in my hands and shrug my shoulders. "He didn't do it."

It isn't necessarily a lie...

It was the broken mirror. Sure, he may have slammed me into it—but it wasn't like he intentionally sliced my cheek open.

Not like you did to him.

I can still feel the pain in my hand from clenching the shard. Still see the way the sharp edge pressed against his throat, the red liquid seeping down.

"Jesus Christ, B, what the hell is going on with you?" She asks, pulling me away from my memories. "You seem a million miles away. What happened last night?"

There is no good way to answer that question.

Oh, yeah, Mallory. I allowed myself to be completely and utterly stripped naked by a stranger in a carnival, both literally and figuratively. He screwed my brains out all over that fucking place. He degraded me, tied me up, locked me in a cage, and dragged me across the floor like a human-sized doll. And you know what? I fucking loved it.

My better sense tells me that admission probably wouldn't go over well. Instead, I settle on a half-truth.

"We talked, got to know each other. I was very... vulnerable with him. Jackson is good at breaking down walls, I guess."

Breaking them. Demolishing them like a wrecking ball. To-may-toe, to-mah-toe.

"So what, you just spilled your guts to him over some popcorn and then went home? You're so full of shit." Mallory's eyes are like molten lava, the heat coming from her gaze staggering. "And let me guess, you tripped on something walking to your car and that's how you fucked up your face. God, I can't believe this."

I set the latte down on the small bistro table beside us and let out a breath.

"Mal, I love you, but back off. Okay? I don't have the energy for this inquisition. My mind is already spinning out of control enough as it is and the last thing I need is you grilling me."

Her eyes narrow and I know she has no intention of letting me off.

"Look, I'm going to head home. I've got a ton to get done and my head is pounding." I take a step toward her and wrap my arms around her stiff body. "I'll call you later, kay?"

I don't wait for her rebuttal, instead turning on my heel and getting the hell out of there.

I can't explain what happened last night when I don't even understand it myself.

The deal was one night. One night only.

But Jackson had stolen something from me. In the process of breaking me apart he'd taken a piece and held on to it. I can almost feel him turning it over in his calloused hands.

For once in my life, one night may not be enough.

His words echo in my mind.

I think I'd stolen a piece of him, too.

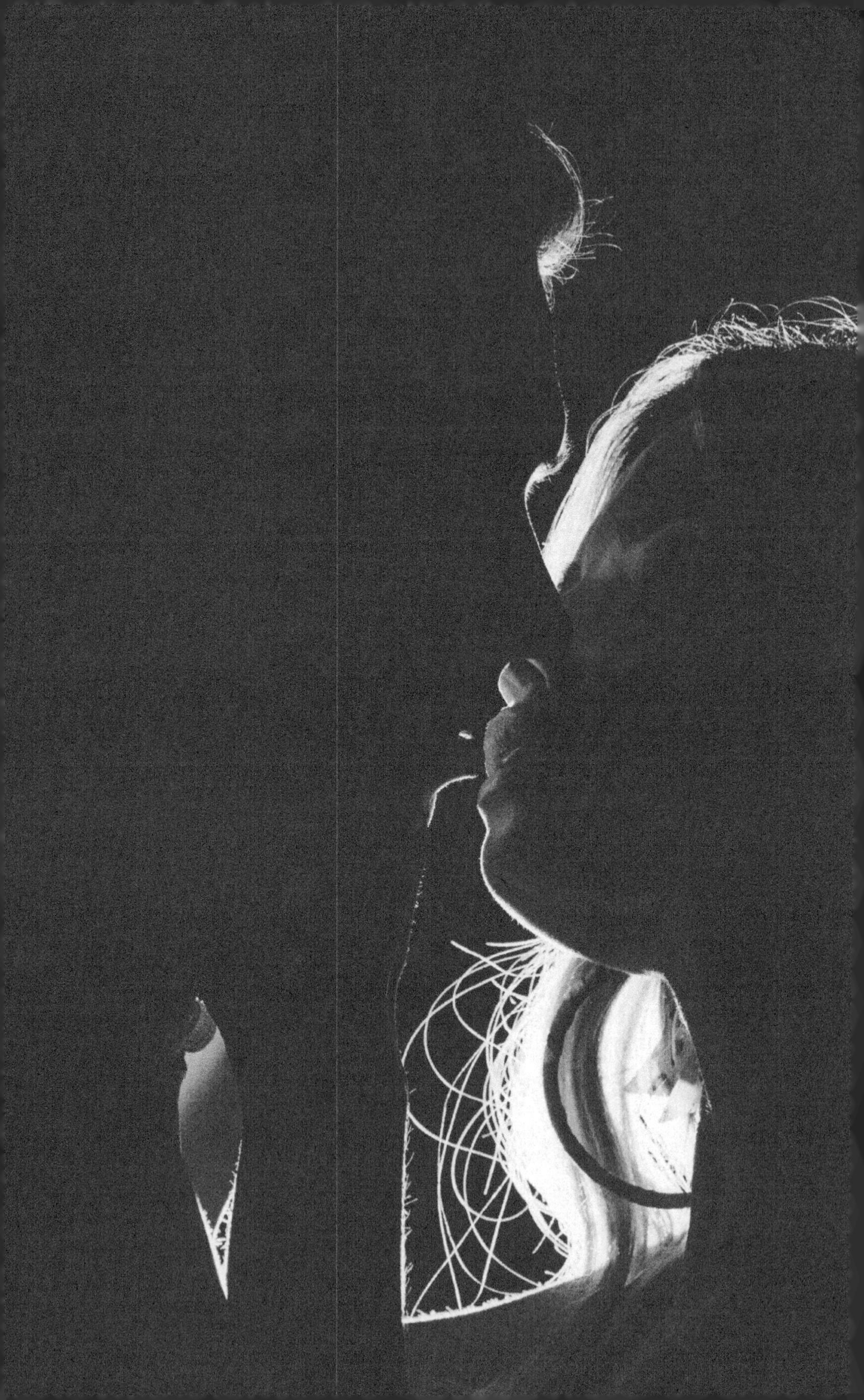

Epilogue

Blair

One month later...

I run my fingers over the scar on my cheek. Feeling the slightly raised line has become somewhat of a comfort.

You would think that any reminder of my night with Jackson would be something I'd want to push as far out of my memory as possible, but for some strange reason it's the complete opposite.

I find myself clinging to those reminders, even though there aren't many. Just the scar and his sweatshirt. The sweatshirt that I haven't washed since that night because it smells like him.

When I slide the material over my body and curl up in bed it almost feels like he's here with me. The only difference? This fucking sweatshirt can't sink its claws into my mind and twist me up like a pretzel. It can't cut me open with its cruel words and then stitch me back up with its touch.

Those are things only *he* can do.

I shouldn't want him like this. He shouldn't be what consumes my every waking thought and my nightmares.

All I can give you is one night, but we can make it one that you will never forget.

Why should I settle for one night? Why does Jackson get to make all the rules?

Hell, he broke his own more times than I can count.

My feet are moving before I have time to flip the switch and turn the rational part of my brain back on.

Fuck the rules, and fuck the consequences. What's the worst that could happen? He says no? That leaves me no worse off than I am right now.

At least I could see him again, even if it is just long enough for him to tell me to fuck off.

What can I say? I'm a sucker for punishment apparently.

My stomach turns over when the bright lights of the looming Ferris wheel come into view. I'm not sure if it's nerves over seeing Jackson again or the fact that I haven't eaten anything since breakfast.

I didn't exactly plan to hop in my car and drive four hours to some small town the next state over. I also didn't think to stop and grab something quick to eat on the way.

The smell wafting from each of the food carts makes my mouth water, but I don't have time to stop. I am a woman on a mission, and that mission does not include a foot-long corn dog.

The layout of the carnival is similar, though not exactly the same as when they were in my hometown. This place is more of an open field than a true event space. I keep my eyes laser-focused on each of the attractions as I make my way down the walkway.

Carnies yell for me to step right up and throw darts at a wall of balloons or shoot a water gun into a spiraled target for the chance to win a stuffed animal. I keep my gaze straight ahead, not giving any off them the time of day.

Shifty's comes into view and my heart rate skyrockets.

An empty metal chair sits right before the entrance. I was fully expecting to see Jackson there, leaned back with his black combat boots crossed at the ankles. His arms stretched out behind his head, a look of pure disinterest painted on his sinfully gorgeous face.

I pull the strand of red tickets from my back pocket and tear off two, rubbing my fingers over the thin paper as I wait for him to return.

An older man's voice says something I can't quite make out from inside the dark building, and when he comes into view I can't hide the tidal wave of disappointment that slams into me.

The man gives me a toothy grin and tips his hat when our eyes lock.

"Got a patron, boy," he calls back to the darkness.

"Fun house is closed."

The sound of Jackson's voice makes my skin heat up like I'm suddenly standing way too close to a fire.

The man shrugs before trudging off back toward the other attractions.

I take the soft, fleshy meat of my inner cheek in my teeth. My feet are cemented to the ground and for some reason I can't seem to come up with a single word to say out loud.

I see him, finally, as he ducks under the curtains that hang above the entrance. He doesn't glance in my direction, his focus on whatever seems to be wrong with the fun house. The lights are off and no music is playing, which is probably why there is not a single soul in line for it.

I shift my weight from one foot to the other and the gravel underneath my shoe crunches.

"Didn't you hear me?" Jackson says in an exasperated huff. "Fun house is closed. Piece of shit lost power and I can't send anyone in."

He sends his boot into the metal wall and lets out a string of expletives that would have at one time have made me blush, but not anymore. Instead, I can't help but giggle.

"What the hell is your—" he starts before whipping his head around to confront whoever the asshole is laughing at his frustration.

"Blair?"

My name dripping from his lips is like an intoxicating drug. The perfect aphrodisiac.

"Hi."

Hi? I drive four hours to see this man and all I can come up with to say is hi? Jesus.

His dark eyes are filled with questions.

"What the fuck are you doing here?"

Nice to see you too, dear.

I hold out the tickets and he knits his brows. "I heard this is the best attraction at the carnival."

He shakes his head. "Cut the shit, Blair. I asked you a question. What the fuck are you doing here?"

I blow out a breath and shrug my shoulders. "I–"

He runs a hand through his black locks and takes a step toward me.

I'm trying to find the words but my brain is not firing on all cylinders. Instead it's sputtering and backfiring and I'm fucking stuck.

"You can't just come here. We had a deal. One night. One night, and then you go back to your princess castle, and I move on with my life."

Heat rises to my cheeks, and not the good kind of heat.

"What if I don't want to go back to my castle, Jackson. What if that one night with you made me realize that I can't fucking stand being that girl anymore?"

He throws his arms outwards and looks at me like I've just said the most ridiculous thing he's ever heard. Like I've just told him I was abducted by aliens or brainwashed by the government.

"Jesus, fuck. This is why there are rules, Blair."

Now I'm the one flailing around like a mad woman.

"To hell with your rules, Jackson! It's not like you followed them anyway. I can't stop thinking about you, about what we did. I can still feel your hands all over my fucking body. Your mouth on my skin and your cock filling me up. You're like a goddamn parasite that's leeched its way into my brain and it's killing me!"

For once I'm the one shutting him up. He's completely speechless.

"I don't want it to just be one night. I want to feel like that over and over again. I want you to break me apart until there is nothing left of the girl I used to be. I'm not done fucking playing the game, and I don't think you are either."

I wait for him to give me any sort of indication on how he's feeling about my little declaration, but he gives me nothing. Instead he stands there, gawking at me like I belong in one of the sideshow acts.

"God, Jackson. Say something."

He turns his back to me and for a moment I think he's going to bolt. That he's going to leave me standing here like some wounded puppy he doesn't have the time or energy to deal with.

I can see his jaw clench, the only giveaway that the wheels in his mind are spinning just as fast as mine.

We are two machines barreling down the tracks at full speed and at any second we will crash into each other, an explosion that would rock this carnival to its core.

It happens so fast. He closes the space between us and grasps my face in his hands, his mouth on mine like a man starved for oxygen and I am his only salvation.

We break apart from each other after what feels like hours and he brushes the hair from my face.

"You got scared, B. That's why the game really ended. I've never done more than one night, princess. I don't do hearts and flowers, and I sure as hell can't be anything like that pathetic frat boy following you around. I know I'm not wired like that. But *you* left. Not me. Is that going to happen again?"

Shaking my head, I can't help but look up at him and smile.

"Maybe we can start with just one more night," he says. "And maybe the night after that. We'll see."

"I'll take whatever you are willing to give me, Jackson."

His hand snakes around the back of my neck and into my hair. He grips it hard in his fist and pulls down so that I'm locked in place.

"You really are a needy little whore, aren't you?"

"Fuck you..." I gasp, reveling in the delicious pain.

Jackson scoffs, pulling even harder.

"Is that what you want, Blair? For me to fuck you?" He grips my throat with his free hand. "Because I intend to. Over and over until you can't see straight. I'm going to enjoy having my favorite toy back where she belongs."

The End...*for now.*

Acknowledgements

What happens when you take an author who has only ever written contemporary romance and pair her with a reader turned first-time author who lives for all things dark and twisty? Well, it seems the answer is this little novella. Co-writing this book was a freaking journey. What started out as a conversation turned into this incredible partnership that I don't think either of us was expecting. Nonetheless, we're here now and not going anywhere. We had so much fun writing this, and can't wait to see what other stories we can cook up for you guys.

To our editor/sensitivity reader/right-hand-man: Havoc Archives, thank you for everything. This novella would never have been a possibility without you. You were, quite literally, there with us every step of the way.

To our ARC team, thank you for giving us a chance on this one and for all the incredible feedback.

And to all our readers, we can't say thank you enough. Thank you for choosing to read our words. It means more than you will ever know.

About the Authors

HARPER ASHLEY IS A COLLEGE STUDENT, MOTHER, AND ROMANCE AUTHOR WHO HAS A UNIQUE ABILITY TO CRAFT CHARACTERS AND RELATIONSHIPS THAT RESONATE DEEPLY WITH READERS. WHEN HARPER ISN'T WRITING, SHE'S WORKING HARD TOWARDS HER DEGREE IN INTERDISCIPLINARY STUDIES WITH A CONCENTRATION IN SOCIAL SCIENCES AND LIBERAL ARTS ALONG WITH A MINOR IN POLITICAL SCIENCE. HER STORYTELLING DISPLAYS HER CREATIVITY, OFTEN ILLUSTRATING CHARACTER-DRIVEN NARRATIVES THAT FOCUS ON RELATABILITY AND EMOTIONAL CONNECTIONS THAT KEEP READERS ASKING FOR MORE.

WREN HAWTHORNE IS A DEGENERATE READER TURNED SPICY AUTHOR WHO LIVES FOR THE DEPRAVED AND DARK. THEY HARBOR A FASCINATION WITH THE FINE LINE THAT'S DRAWN BETWEEN GOOD AND EVIL. BEYOND THE PAGES OF THEIR STORIES, WREN MAINTAINS AN ENIGMATIC PERSONA. THIS ONLY ADDS TO THE ALLURE OF THEIR WORK, LEAVING READERS WONDERING WHO THE SICK AND TWISTED PERSON BEHIND THE WRITING IS. WITH STORIES THAT CONTINUE TO PUSH BOUNDARIES, THEY CREATE NARRATIVES THAT PLUNGE READERS INTO THEIR MOST FORBIDDEN DESIRES. THEIR CHARACTERS ARE DAMAGED, SALACIOUS, AND MORALLY AMBIGUOUS, OFTEN MIRRORING PARTS OF THE AUTHOR THEMSELF.

Made in United States
Orlando, FL
09 November 2024

53480542R00065